Norman Jacobs & Kerry O'Quinn present

# space art

Compiled and written by Ron Miller
Art Director: Robert P. Ericksen
Designer: Phyllis Cayton

Editors: Jon-Michael Reed, Robin Snelson
Art Staff: Laura O'Brien, Susan Stevens
Asst. Publisher: Ira Friedman

## About The Wrap-around Cover:

Saturn, as seen from its moon, Titan, is almost the trademark of Chesley Bonestell. At age ninety, Bonestell is the quintessential astronomical artist. For the cover of SPACE ART, Bonestell visited Titan once again to paint this famous scene, based on the latest scientific findings. He describes the painting: "Constantly and totally cloud-covered, Saturn, seen from its largest satellite, Titan (3,000 miles in diameter), subtends an angle of approximately six degrees from a distance of 759,000 miles. Seen here through a normal visual angle (approximately forty degrees), it covers one-seventh of the sky. Titan is known to be reddish and to hold a thin atmosphere, and is probably covered with patches of frozen atmosphere, or "snow," due to its extreme cold."

**STARLOG PRESS**
O'Quinn Studios, Inc.
Norman Jacobs/Kerry O'Quinn
475 Park Avenue South
New York, NY 10016

# Preface

Neil Armstrong was *not* the first person to set foot on the Moon. Hundreds of thousands of men, women, and children had already been there and were watching that historic television broadcast in 1969 just to see if NASA's discoveries would live up to the visions we had already seen.

Earlier visions had been supplied, not by scientists, but by artists — by Chesley Bonestell, Fred Freeman, and Rolf Klep, among others. These painters and illustrators had engaged in an important human process called extrapolation.

Strictly defined, extrapolation means to infer an *unknown* from something that *is* known. In the visual arts, the process of inferring leads to more than just guesses and reasoned conclusions — it leads to realistic pictures. Viewers can do more than appreciate the abstract speculation of scientists and astronomers, we can *see* them in concrete reality.

Space artists make it possible for us to walk on the Moon.

Good extrapolation requires a keen mind — one that can understand the frontiers of knowledge in the various sciences involved, and can fill in the gaps with reasoned assumptions that are not out of line with the known facts.

And, of course, the professional space artist must also be a master of rendering techniques and possess a vivid sense of imagination, of wonder, and of the Romantic spirit.

If one saw a classified job ad that listed the necessary skills for a space artist position, most good artists would find that they need not bother to apply.

Space artists are special people, miles above the arbitrary splashers and dribblers who clutter Madison Avenue galleries, yet the artistic abilities of space artists have never received the serious attention and praise from critics that they deserve. And their cultural contributions — their inspiration to scientists and to the public — have likewise remained unrecognized.

It is toward correcting that error that this book is dedicated — the first ever devoted exclusively to space art.

*Kerry O'Quinn / 1978*

# Contents

Artist Index . . . . . . . . . . . . . . . . . . . . . . . . . . . . . . . . . . 7
Introduction: In the Beginning . . . . . . . . . . . . . . . . . . . . . . 8
The Archaeology of Space Art . . . . . . . . . . . . . . . . . . . . . . 10
The Masters of Space Art
   Chesley Bonestell . . . . . . . . . . . . . . . . . . . . . . . . . . . . 20
   Bob McCall . . . . . . . . . . . . . . . . . . . . . . . . . . . . . . . . . 30
   Ludek Pesek . . . . . . . . . . . . . . . . . . . . . . . . . . . . . . . . 38
   Lucien Rudaux . . . . . . . . . . . . . . . . . . . . . . . . . . . . . . 44
The Big Back Yard
   Mercury . . . . . . . . . . . . . . . . . . . . . . . . . . . . . . . . . . . 50
   Venus . . . . . . . . . . . . . . . . . . . . . . . . . . . . . . . . . . . . . 56
   Earth . . . . . . . . . . . . . . . . . . . . . . . . . . . . . . . . . . . . . 58
   The Moon . . . . . . . . . . . . . . . . . . . . . . . . . . . . . . . . . . 62
   Mars . . . . . . . . . . . . . . . . . . . . . . . . . . . . . . . . . . . . . 70
   Jupiter . . . . . . . . . . . . . . . . . . . . . . . . . . . . . . . . . . . . 80
   Uranus . . . . . . . . . . . . . . . . . . . . . . . . . . . . . . . . . . . . 88
   Neptune . . . . . . . . . . . . . . . . . . . . . . . . . . . . . . . . . . . 90
   Pluto . . . . . . . . . . . . . . . . . . . . . . . . . . . . . . . . . . . . . 92
Everybody's Favorite Planet: Saturn . . . . . . . . . . . . . . . . . . 94
Comets, Etc. . . . . . . . . . . . . . . . . . . . . . . . . . . . . . . . . . . 108
The Galaxy and Its Worlds . . . . . . . . . . . . . . . . . . . . . . . . 112
How We'll Get There: The Hardware Artists . . . . . . . . . . . . 122
The Universe and the Imagination . . . . . . . . . . . . . . . . . . . 140
The NASA Fine Arts Program . . . . . . . . . . . . . . . . . . . . . . 148
The Great 1951 Space Program . . . . . . . . . . . . . . . . . . . . 164
About Some of the Artists . . . . . . . . . . . . . . . . . . . . . . . . . 176
Where to See Space Art . . . . . . . . . . . . . . . . . . . . . . . . . . 182
Where to Buy Space Art . . . . . . . . . . . . . . . . . . . . . . . . . . 184
The Making of a Space Painting . . . . . . . . . . . . . . . . . . . . 186
Selected Bibliography . . . . . . . . . . . . . . . . . . . . . . . . . . . . 190
Acknowledgements . . . . . . . . . . . . . . . . . . . . . . . . . . . . . . 191
About the Author . . . . . . . . . . . . . . . . . . . . . . . . . . . . . . . 192

# Artist Index

Arlt, Paul................................**163**

Bayard, Emile................................11
Beard, Dan................................12,**17**
Bensusen, Sally................................**88**, 176
Berkey, John................................122, 185
Bittinger, Charles................................17, **19**
Bolton, Scriven................................15, **16**, 20, 44
Bonestell, Chesley........cover, 9, 10, 14, 15, 17, 20, **21-29**, 44,
**58, 63, 66-67, 76, 81, 85, 99, 102, 120,** 122, **132, 137,**
164, **166-167, 169, 173,** 183, 185-186
Brown, Howard V................................**87**
Buinis, Lonny................................**103**
Butler, Howard Russell................................15, **59**

Calle, Paul................................**156-157, 160, 162, 183**
Clark, John................................**130**
Clement, Hal................................**114-115,** 186
Coggins, Jack................................**67, 135, 138-139,** 176
Crane, Ray................................**140,** 176
Cunningham, James................................**145,** 176

Davis, Don................................**60, 74-75, 102, 115, 119,** 122, 177
deNeuvill, A................................11
DiFate, Vincent................................**136,** 177, 185
Dixon, Don........**56, 62, 64-65, 80, 92-93, 107, 119,** 177, 185
Dodd, Lamar................................153

Egge, David................................**57, 87,** 177
Emerson, Gilbert................................17

Foss, Chris................................122
Freeman, Fred...**134, 153,** 164, **170, 174-175,** 177-179, **188-189**

Hardy, David................................**110-111, 112-113, 124-125,** 178, 185
Hardy, Paul................................12, **81**
Hartmann, William K................................9, **68,** 178, 183, 185
Hervat, James................................**51, 77, 98, 107,** 178-179, 185
Hunter, Mel................................**68, 141**

Jamieson, Mitchell................................**161**
Jane, Fred T................................12

Kent, Rockwell................................17
Klep, Rolf................................164, **168, 170-172,** 178
Krasyk, Francis J................................**151**

Lehr, Paul................................**142-143,** 179, 183
Leigh, W.R................................**13**

Lothers, John................................17

MacDonall, Angus................................**10**
McCall, Bob................................30, **31-37,** 183
Mead, Syd................................**128,** 185
Meigs, John................................**157**
Miller, Ron........**72, 78-79, 86, 94, 99, 106, 116-117,** 185, 192
Miller, Tom................................**89,** 179
Mion, Pierre................................122, **133, 139,** 179, 183
Moreaux, Abbe Theophile................................15, 44, **95,** 179
Morghen, Filippo................................11
Mullins, Jay................................**126**

Nasmyth, James................................12, 44, **67**

Olson, John................................**126**
Palmstrom, William................................17, 19, **58, 129**
Paul, Frank R................................15, **136**
Pesek, Ludek........19, 38, **39-43, 52-53, 70-71, 73, 90-91,**
**96-97, 100-101, 104-106, 108,** 183,185-186
Phillipoteaux, P................................11, **15, 102**
Pitz, Henry C................................**154-155**

Rauschenberg, Robert................................**149,** 153, 183
Rockwell, Norman................................**158-159,** 179, 183
Rose, Sheila................................**54-55, 144,** 179, 183, 185
Rudaux, Lucien........14-15, 19, 20, 44, **45-49, 57, 61, 66, 68,**
**76, 102,** 179

Schaller, Adolf................................**82-83,** 179, 183, 185
Schneeman, Charles................................17
Schoenherr, John................................**120,** 179
Schomburg, Alex................................**103, 118,** 180
Smith, R.A................................12, **61, 131, 135,** 180
Sokolov, Andrei................................**127, 147,** 180, 185
Solovioff, Nicholas................................**160**
Stevens, D. Owen................................**121**

Watt-Geiger, Denise................................**123,** 181
Weymouth, George................................**160**
Whelan, Mike................................**144,** 181
Williams, Leroy................................**132**
Willis, John................................**152**
Wimmer, Helmut................................**146,** 181
Wood, Stanley L................................12, **18**
Wright, H. Seppings................................**12**
Wyeth, James................................**150**

*Note: Bold face page numbers indicate art reproductions.*

# In The Beginning

Unlike many space artists who have picked up astronomy on the way, I did it backwards, by becoming a professional astronomer (Ph.D. astronomy, M.S. geology, B.S. physics) who picked up painting on the way.

Like many space artists and scientists, I was influenced as a teenager in the 1950s by the Chesley Bonestell images appearing in magazines and in books like *The Conquest of Space.* I am convinced that visionaries such as Bonestell, by creating images of places where humanity could go before we had the technology to go there, played a subtle but major role in getting us off the Earth. They affected a generation of youngsters who later became the scientists and technicians that turned the dream into reality. Someone had to create the original image—the idea. Today's space artists play that role for the next century.

It is interesting that many scientists who may have started off as youngsters, impressed in this visual way, have evolved into scientists who have lost a sensory feel for their work. Schools and careers in science and technology today (but not always in the past or perhaps future) tend to train students away from visual dreams, because the greatest success in making workable machines and theories has come from the analytic approach of breaking systems down into mathematically analyzable parts. It has to be this way for us to build things. But that doesn't mean that our visual imaginations need to atrophy.

Painting forces us to synthesize everything we know from science, nature, and art to produce the scenes that our instruments measure. It is bad enough that the public has a hard time visualizing the extraordinary scenes that exist elsewhere in space. But even the scientists who discover these scenes apparently often don't visualize them.

I have had the experience of attending scientific meetings where new phenomena were announced and talking to the discoverer (who may have announced, for example, a luminous glow with a brightness measured in some obscure scientific units). I said, "What would that actually look like to the human eye if you could stand there and see it? Is it bright enough to be visible?" No answer. The question had never even occurred to my friend.

Perhaps it is a state of elevated scientific grace when the effects you measure are so detached from ordinary reality that you don't even know if they'd be detectable by the body—but, I don't think so. Space artists of the realist school have a role to play. They can make us aware of what we are discovering out there. And, space artists of the fantastic school make us aware of unimagined possibilities.

WILLIAM K. HARTMANN
Senior Scientist
Planetary Science Institute
Tucson, Arizona

*Artist unknown, from* The Book of Popular Science, *1924.*

# The Archaeology of Space Art

*Angus MacDonall, from* Drowsy, *1914.*

Even the most realistic portrait artist, if he's creative, brings a vivid imagination to his studio, along with paints and brushes. The goal of the artist is to look at reality, to form a personal impression of it, and to develop the skills necessary to render the impression in objective terms. The artist is constantly weighing the photographic rendering of reality against the recreation he can construct through his own imagination. And the balance he selects between naturalism and imagination often becomes the artist's identifiable style.

The artist is normally allowed great latitude in his adherence to reality. If the flowers in his studio still-life are wilted, he is permitted to paint them as if they were freshly cut. Personal selectivity is a key element in good painting and gives art an emotional power that photography can never equal. Yet, there is one category of art in which departures from reality oppose the purpose of the art.

The purpose is to visualize a part of reality which is "unseeable," and the person who does this is the scientific artist.

The two sciences which the scientific artist pursues are paleontology (with its inability to see anything but petrified bones) and astronomy (with its numbing mathematics and interminable star fields which are incomprehensible to anyone but the scientists involved). Both sciences need to have their subject matter visualized in realistic, concrete terms—not just laboratory symbols and other mumbo-jumbo.

When the scientific artist creates an accurate vision of the unseen objects, he not only provides inspiration to those working in the field, but he forms a method of communication to the rest of the world: the non-scientific public. In the case of astronomical art, there is little question that the taxpayers of the world were rallied behind the space program largely due to popular illustrated magazine articles and books—like the *Collier's* and *Life* series of the '50s and the now-classic books by Chesley Bonestell, with text by Wernher von Braun, Willy Ley, and others.

The astronomical artists of the last few decades had as much to do with the success of the space effort as any technical advances. Just as early American artists showed the public views of the unconquered West and helped propel interest in exploration and expansion (as artists of vision and realistic imagination always point the way), so, too, astronomical artists have shown the public what the unseen planets, moons, comets, and distant reaches of the galaxy might look like when we are able to be there in person.

And, as a result, just as the field of astronomy has produced eminent scientists, it has also produced several great artists.

Before the time of Jules Verne, flights to the Moon were visually depicted with the aid of geese and demons. The moon environment contained a world of pumpkin-houses (Filippo Morghen, in a picture-book engraved in the late eight-eenth century) or mountains of ruby (Richard Locke's *The Moon Hoax*, 1835). Even according to the limited astronomical knowledge of the time, there were no visions of what could or should be expected. Rather, the visions were simply allegorical outlets for the authors' and artists' social, religious, or occult beliefs.

The famous stories of travel to the Moon by Cyrano deBergerac and Edgar Allan Poe were solely vehicles for satire on contemporary society. Johann Kepler's *Somnium* (1634) demonstrated that this wasn't necessary. His *method* of getting to the Moon is supernatural. (Space-travel stories of every age employ means of travel that are best accepted by the intended audience. For example, Verne employed a giant cannon to launch his manned projectile, because the rocket was in such an early stage of development that none of his readers would have believed rockets to be realistic.) But Kepler's Moon is not supernatural.

"Night is fifteen or sixteen days long, and dreadful with uninterrupted shadow," Kepler wrote. His Moon is similar to our world except that mountains are much higher and more rugged, with deep valleys and fissures. Kepler was also aware of the Moon's extreme climate, the weightlessness and the airlessness of space, and was the first writer to propose lunar inhabitants with a biology to suit their environment. Had *Somnium* been illustrated, it might have provided us with the first true astronomical art.

The first space art appeared in 1865 with the illustrations by Emile Bayard and A. de Neuvill for Jules Verne's novel, *From the Earth to the Moon*. As mentioned, there had been imaginary views of other worlds, and even of space flight, before this. But until Verne's book appeared, these views all had been heavily colored by mysticism rather than science.

The illustrations accompanying *From the Earth to the Moon* and its sequel, *A Trip Around the Moon*, were the first artistic impressions of space ever created strictly according to scientific fact. This was no accident. Verne, a meticulous researcher of facts, was in the habit of overseeing the illustrations of his novels. His prime interest in creating his stories was to present a series of scientific or geographical facts which were sugar-coated with a good story. And he realized that the illustrations that went with his stories must conform to fact as well. For these books, Verne even had a lunar map specially drawn by Beer and Maedler, the leading selenographers of the day.

In 1877, Verne published *Off On a Comet*, with illustrations by P. Phillipoteaux of such scenes as Jupiter and its moons as seen from a passing asteroid and Saturn's rings as seen from the surface of that planet. In the novel itself, there is a passage evocative of the following century of space art:

"To any observer stationed on the planet, between the extremes of lat. 45 degrees on either side of the equator, these wonderful rings would present various strange phenomena. Sometimes they would appear as an illuminated arch, with the shadow of Saturn passing over it like the hour-hand over a dial; at other times they would be like a semi-aureole of light. Very often, too, for periods of several years, daily eclipses of the sun must occur through the interpositions of this triple ring.

"Truly, with the constant rising and setting of satellites, some with bright discs at their full, others like silver crescents, in quadrature, as well as by the encircling rings, the aspect of the heavens from the surface of Saturn must be as impressive as it is gorgeous."

In 1874, James Nasmyth and James Carpenter published their classic study of the Earth's satellite, *The Moon*. A large and lavishly illustrated volume, its numerous plates were reproductions of photographs of plaster models of portions of the lunar surface, seen both telescopically from Earth and as they would appear to an observer on the Moon. The models, and the one or two paintings in the book, were all created by James Nasmyth, one of the pioneers of lunar origin theory.

The year 1887 saw the beginning of the *Cassell's Family Magazine* serial, "Letters from the Planets," by W.S. Lach-Szyrma (completed in 1893). It is the story of a tour that visits the Sun, Mercury, Mars, and the moons of Jupiter. The series had illustrations by Paul Hardy, which reflect the astronomical facts and theories of the time. For example, it was thought that the Sun's heat was maintained by the impact of the millions of meteorites that must hourly fall into it. The serial, "Stories of Other Worlds," by George Griffith (later published in book form as *Honeymoon in Space*) appeared in 1900 and was profusely illustrated by Stanley L. Wood. Once again, planetary surfaces are shown in the light of contemporary science. However, a visit to the Moon is shown in two excellent illustrations of the hero and heroine in very realistic space suits, exploring a convincing lunar surface.

For a period of years at the end of the last century, artist and writer Fred T. Jane produced a series of illustrations for *Pall Mall* magazine, entitled "Guesses at Futurity." Some of these, such as "Gold Mining in the Mountains of the Moon," are remarkably similar to the moon colonies pictured sixty years later by British Interplanetary Society artist R.A. Smith.

*A Journey in Other Worlds* by John Jacob Astor was illustrated by Dan Beard (who founded the Boy Scouts) and published in 1894. The book begins with a tour of the world of 2000 AD (which proves that Astor was a brilliant and pre-

Above: *By H. Seppings Wright, from* Splendour of the Heavens, *1927.*
Right: *By W. R. Leigh, from* Cosmopolitan, *1905.*

scient engineer) and continues to a flight to Jupiter that contains descriptions of that world, which, although wrong by today's science, would do justice to Hal Clement or Arthur C. Clarke. The novel also contains a description of ''Cassandra,'' the tenth, trans-Neptunian planet (Pluto's discovery was still over thirty years in the future),that is incredibly prophetic:

''. . . the sun, though brighter, appears no larger than the Earth's evening or morning star. Cassandra has also three large moons; but these, when full, shine with a pale grey light. . . . The temperature at Cassandra's surface is but little above the cold of space, and no water exists in the liquid state, it being as much a solid as liquid or glass. There are rivers and lakes, but these consist of liquefied hydrogen and other gasses, the heavier liquid collected in deep places, and the lighter . . . floating upon it without mixing, as oil on water . . . were there mortal inhabitants on Cassandra, they might build their houses of blocks of oxygen or chlorine . . . and use ice that never melts, in place of glass. . . .

''Though Cassandra's atmosphere, such as it is, is mostly clear . . . the brightness of even the highest moon is less than an earthly twilight, and the stars never cease to shine. The dark base of the rocky cliffs, is washed by a frigid tide, but there is scarcely a sound, for the pebbles cannot be moved by the weightless waves. . . .''

During and immediately following the turn of the century, many popular books on astronomy were published and illustrated with space art. The most outstanding illustrator of such books, Lucien Rudaux, was also the first genuine astronomical artist. Rudaux (1874-1947) was both an artist and a professional astronomer. He wrote and illustrated a number of texts, such as the authoritative (and still in print) *Larousse Encyclopedia of Astronomy*. For his work, Rudaux received many awards, including the Legion of Honor, and more recently, a Martian crater was named after him (see Masters of Space Art chapter).

Although Chesley Bonestell was later to make the concept of a craggy moonscape the most popular image, the Moon, as Rudaux painted it in the 1920s and '30s, was a bland, rolling landscape, with rounded, sloping mountains. In fact, many of Rudaux's lunar scenes look uncannily like

*''Magic has paved the way for science.''*
— Sir James Frazer
The Golden Bough

Apollo photographs. Ironically, Rudaux wrote in 1926:

"It is astonishing . . . what phantastic representations have been drawn of the landscapes of this lunar world. Numerous astronomical treatises have represented them as embellished with mountains and peaks made of jagged sugar loafs, at the feet of which are heaped numerous small vatlike formations having the appearance of volcanic molehills."

*The Illustrated London News* of the 1920s was to space art what *Life* was later to become in the '50s. Rudaux was a frequent contributor, as was Scriven Bolton, who began the technique of constructing model landscapes set against painted backgrounds. His work can be found in many books, notably the lavishly illustrated, two-volume *Splendour of the Heavens* (1927). He was joined in this book by the Abbe Moreux, whose work dates from the late 1800s. Although Bolton and Moreux did excellent work, their many mistakes inspired a young artist, who had been executing architectural renderings for the *Illustrated London News,* to "indulge in space painting." The young artist was Chesley Bonestell (see Masters of Space Art chapter).

An American artist of this era, Howard Russell Butler, N.A. (1836-1934), produced many painterly space scenes. To render his canvases of solar eclipses, Butler would even travel on solar eclipse expeditions to witness the actual events. Many of his paintings are in the collections of the American Museum of Natural History and the Smithsonian Institution.

*By P. Phillipoteaux, from* Off on a Comet, *1877.*

Frank R. Paul (1884-1964) produced an unbelievable volume of work during his career—primarily for Hugo Gernsback's many publications, particularly *Science and Invention* and *Amazing.* He was trained as an engineer and architect, and his hardware (if nothing else) was drawn convincingly and authoritatively, although always with an odd flavor of art nouveau. His astronomical work was always a little more imaginative than anything else painted in the field at the time. Paul produced

Left: *By Scriven Bolton, from* Splendour of the Heavens, *1927.*
Top: *Artist unknown, from* A Study of the Sky, *1896.*
Above: *By Dan Beard, from* Journey in Other Worlds, *1894.*

some excellent work, such as the illustrations for *Science and Invention* which depict some of the strange visual effects of Saturn's rings.

For the November 1, 1937, issue of *Life* magazine, Rockwell Kent provided four stylish lithographs, illustrating as many possible ends for our Earth. Kent was one of this nation's most highly regarded artist-illustrators, still famous for his classic artwork for *Moby Dick,* Boccaccio's *Decameron,* and his own *N by E.* His lithographs for *Life* anticipate Bonestell's 1953 *End of the World.* Coincidentally, Chesley Bonestell once collaborated on an eighty-foot mural with Kent, in Maine, circa 1920.

For the April, 1939, issue of *Astounding,* Charles Schneeman created one of the finest of all pre-Bonestell astronomical paintings. During his long career he produced many superb astronomical cover paintings. The illustrations by Charles Bittinger for the July, 1939, *National Geographic* show how far ahead even the science-fiction pulps of the '30s were in the accurate depiction of astronomical concepts. Bittinger's paintings were among the very first astronomical art to appear in a nationally distributed popular magazine and were described as "combining a fine sense of color values and artistic composition with a painstaking effort to achieve scientific accuracy." But with one or two possible exceptions, they are rather crudely done and the science is only slightly better. Bittinger later did other space and scientific subjects for the *Geographic.* He covered a solar eclipse expedition, was official artist for Task Force One, and recorded the Task Force's first atomic bomb experiments in the Pacific in the late '40s.

*National Geographic* redeemed itself two decades later by way of the art that accompanied the article, "How Man-Made Satellites Can Affect Our Lives," in the December, 1957, issue. The art was by staff illustrators John Lothers, William Palmstrom, and Gilbert Emerson. These artists created some of the most beautiful paintings of satellites in

orbit yet published (at a time when only the Soviets had a satellite in space). Palmstrom had also, in another issue, painted the Earth as it would appear in space: probably the best and most accurate such painting done since Lucien Rudaux's similar attempts in the '30s. Of course, it was also the *Geographic* that first introduced Ludek Pesek to American audiences, in 1970.

Astronomical art blossomed after the 1950s. In the years immediately before and following the launch of Sputnik I (1957), the space art that appeared in magazines, such as *Collier's, This Week,* and *Coronet,* and in books, such as *The Conquest of Space* and Arthur C. Clarke's *Exploration of Space* (which was a 1951 Book-of-the-Month Club selection), helped convince the public that space exploration was far from a fantasy and that it was well within the reach of contemporary science and engineering. Beyond the question of hardware, realistic and accurate paintings of other worlds showed that the moons and planets were not as insubstantial as fuzzy astronomical photographs made them seem, but were genuine worlds in their own right.

There are more artists illustrating space subjects today than all those in the past combined. This is due partly to the increased interest in space travel and the broad range the subject allows the artistic imagination.

Modern space artists have both an easier and, at the same time, more difficult job than the space artists of a generation ago. More discoveries have been made about the nature of our neighboring planets in the last decade than in all the previous history of astronomy. Contemporary artists certainly have more factual material to draw upon, yet this abundance also limits them. We *know* what the surface of Mars looks like now—there is far less leeway for the artist's own imagination. The phrase "artist's impression" attached to a space painting no longer means an imaginary guess. □

Above: *The Earth, seen from the Moon's surface, by Charles Bittinger, N.A. (copyright National Geographic Society).*
Opposite: *By Stanley Wood, from* Honeymoon in Space, *1900.*

# The Masters of Space Art

When Chesley Bonestell was born, the Wright Brothers were only seventeen and twenty-one, and Robert Goddard, the inventor of the liquid-fueled rocket, was a mere six years of age. The hottest news in aviation was the flight of the first gasoline-powered balloon, and Jules Verne still had half his writing career ahead of him. H.G. Wells was not quite twenty-two and as yet unpublished. Ninety years later, Bonestell is still hard at work. His lifetime embraces the first manned airplane flight and the first Moon landings. He was not the first artist to work with astronomy, but the extraordinarily high level of quality and integrity in his work, as well as its wide-spread visibility, raised astronomical art to the level of a distinct artistic genre.

Bonestell's original training—and first love—was architecture. He began his career as an architectural renderer and designer, with several prominent San Francisco homes to his credit. In the 1920s, he worked for the *Illustrated London News*, doing renderings of famous buildings. It was then that he was first introduced to the space art of Scriven Bolton and Lucien Rudaux. After returning to the U.S., Bonestell returned to architectural designing and worked on such projects as the Supreme Court Building in Washington, D.C., the Chrysler Building in New York City, and San Francisco's Golden Gate Bridge. Using his specialized knowledge of perspective and the highly representational painting techniques architectural rendering required, he went to work in the late 1930s as a special-effects matte painter in Hollywood. His artwork can be seen in such films as *Citizen Kane, Only Angels Have Wings, The Magnificent Ambersons, The Hunchback of Notre Dame,* and *How Green Was My Valley.*

In 1944, *Life* published a series of paintings showing the planet Saturn as seen from some of its satellites. These were the first printed astronomical paintings by Bonestell. He used his knowledge of camera angles, perspective, and a life-long interest in astronomy to produce the most plausibly realistic portrayals of other worlds yet done. This immediately led to a virtual full-time career in space art. He provided technical advice and special-effects artwork for the classic science-fiction films *War of the Worlds, Destination Moon,* and *The Conquest of Space.* He provided much of the art for the great *Collier's* series on space flight, which were later transformed into the classic books, *Conquest of the Moon, The Exploration of Mars,* and *Across the Space Frontier* (authored by Wernher von Braun, Fred Whipple, Willy Ley, and others). His earliest astronomical paintings were gathered into his first book, with text by Willy Ley, *The Conquest of Space,* a best-seller in 1949 and now a highly-prized collector's item.

He painted several murals, notably a 10' x 40' panorama of the lunar surface for the Boston Museum of Science, which is now in the National Air and Space Museum in Washington, D.C. He has had numerous one-man shows, including two at the Smithsonian Institution—a very rare distinction. He has received the Science Fiction Special Achievement Award, the British Interplanetary Society Special Award and Medallion for lifetime accomplishments in space exploration, and the Dorothea Kumke Roberts Award from the Astronomical Society of the Pacific.

Bonestell's career has not only documented the development of space exploration, but has, in very large and unique measure, contributed to its final success. The persuasive, photographic realism of his paintings, combined with a nineteenth-century romanticism and sense of wonder, helped to convince a skeptical nation of taxpayers that the exploration of space was not only a very beautiful dream, but that it was well within the grasp of reality. □

# CHESLEY BONESTELL

*The surface of Mercury, from the classic book,* The Conquest of Space, *1949. By Chesley Bonestell (Frederick C. Durant, III Collection, courtesy of the artist).*

This painting was done for the Collier's space series. It shows a fleet of
von Braun-designed spacecraft in Earth orbit, just before leaving for Mars. The
small spacecraft carry personnel, and the large-winged craft are
intended for the descent to the Martian surface. Only the small ships will make
the round trip. By Chesley Bonestell (Adams Collection, courtesy of the artist).

Right: *Saturn, as seen from its largest moon, Titan.*
Below: *Painted for the Life Magazine series, ''The World We Live In'':*
*Earth's continents congeal, incessantly bombarded by meteorites.*
*On the horizon looms a swollen moon (Starlog Collection).*
Bottom: *Painted for the cover of Man and the Moon, 1961: the exploration*
*of the Jura Mountains on the Sinus Iridum, as seen from a crater in Mare*
*Imbrium. All by Chesley Bonestell (courtesy of the artist).*

Top: *A team of astronauts explore the lunar crater Copernicus (Ron Miller Collection).*
Above: *A lunar landscape (Smithsonian Institution Collection).*
Left: *A ground station on Mars, for* The Exploration of Mars, *1956 (Smithsonian Institution Collection).*
All by Chesley Bonestell *(courtesy of the artist).*

Overleaf: *Saturn, as it appears in the sky of its satellite, Iapetus. Although nine times further from Iapetus than our Moon is from Earth, giant Saturn still appears four times larger than a terrestrial full Moon. First published in* Life, *1944. By Chesley Bonestell (courtesy of the artist).*

Bob McCall, born in 1919 in Columbus, Ohio, has had a life-long interest in art and aerospace subjects. As a child he liked to draw airplanes and armored knights and remembers: "I liked airplanes, because they made a lot of noise and were dramatic and moved fast—all the things kids like airplanes for. The knights in armor, now that I look back, are not unlike astronauts in space suits, and represent some of the same things to me: man adventurous, risking everything, facing new challenges. . . ."

McCall studied art on a scholarship at the Columbus College of Art and Design and the Art Institute of Chicago. During World War II, he was an Army Air Corps bombardier instructor, flying B-17s, B-21s, and B-24s. He has maintained close ties with the Air Force, travelling around the world to produce documentary art for the Air Force's art collection. After his military service, he worked as an illustrator with Bielefeld Studios in Chicago and then the Charles E. Cooper Studios in New York. In addition to his aviation and space work (and he currently specializes—although not exclusively, by any means—in the latter), he has worked in a wide range of advertising, industrial, and general editorial and story illustration in most of the major magazines. Like many of today's top illustrators, some of McCall's first work appeared in SF—one of his first was a cover for *Amazing Quarterly.*

McCall was naturally enthusiastic when the space program began in the 1950s. Contacting *Life* magazine, he began covering not only the infant space efforts, but future concepts as well. That work eventually led to his advertising art for the film, *2001: A Space Odyssey,* which was his springboard to fame within the genre of science fiction and speculative technical art. The originals of these posters are now in the collection of the National Air and Space Museum, where many of his other paintings are exhibited.

McCall produced artwork for a coffee-table volume, with text by Isaac Asimov, titled *Our World in Space,* which illustrated concepts of space exploration and colonization from the very near tomorrow to the very imaginative future. Since *2001,* McCall has been involved in conceptualizations for motion pictures, working very closely in the preproduction stages of science-fiction projects for Walt Disney, Doug Trumbull, and others.

McCall was among the first artists to be invited to take part in NASA's fine arts program and has continued to document the manned space program. One of his newest paintings to join the NASA collection depicts the rollout of the space shuttle *Enterprise.* He has also designed commemorative postage stamps, book jackets, and what must be one of the most-photographed works of art in the nation's capitol: a six-story-high mural for the National Air and Space Museum.  □

# BOB McCALL

*Early settlement of the Moon will be work-horsed by functional, cylindrical spacecraft, as envisioned here by Bob McCall (courtesy of the artist).*

An astronaut activates his
(or her) portable rocket
unit, creating a brilliant
display of light in Earth
orbit. Below are a space
station and advanced
shuttle vehicles. The majesty
of this painting conveys
the artist's spirit of
wonder about outer space.
By Bob McCall (courtesy
of the artist).

Above: *Construction of a Gerard O'Neill-type space habitat around the year 2000, from a cover of Future Magazine, 1978 (Starlog Collection).*
Right: *Vehicles are launched from a futuristic, anti-gravity city, as it hovers over the Grand Canyon. Both by Bob McCall (courtesy of the artist).*

Overleaf: *A spacecraft propelled by detonating atomic bombs in a  spherical chamber. By Bob McCall (courtesy of the artist).*

Ludek Pesek (born 1919) first came to the attention of American readers with his spectacular debut in the August, 1970, *National Geographic* article,"Voyage to the Planets," for which he had provided fifteen color paintings. This was followed by "Journey to Mars" for the same magazine, which included a poster-size reproduction of a painting of a Martian dust storm. He has since appeared in several U.S. publications: *Smithsonian,* again in *National Geographic, Starlog,* and others.

Pesek's art is closer in manner of execution to Lucien Rudaux's than to Chesley Bonestell's. Rather than creating a pseudo-photograph, Pesek paints landscapes in a loose, almost impressionistic manner, which only suggests detail. However, his scenes are so natural-looking, without any appearance of invention or artificiality, that the viewer accepts them as representations of reality. He also possesses one of the most original imaginations of all the astronomical artists. While staying well within the limits of scientific accuracy, he is still able to create new and exciting ways to see subjects that may have been painted a dozen times by other artists.

A Czechoslovakian expatriate now living in Switzerland, Pesek had already attained a European reputation for his award-winning novels and photo-books before his first volume of astronomical paintings, *The Moon and the Planets,* was published. This over-size collection of forty double-page illustrations was translated in Italian, English, Japanese, and Russian, and received an honorable mention at the International Biennial of Illustration in 1966. It was followed by a companion volume in 1967, *Our Planet Earth,* which traced,in forty color paintings, the history of the Earth's surface from its creation to the present day. That year Pesek also wrote his first two science-fiction novels, *Log of a Moon Expedition* and *The Earth is Near.* The two over-size picture books first brought him to the attention of Frederick C. Durant, III, Assistant Director of the Smithsonian Institution's National Air and Space Museum, who in turn introduced Pesek to the *National Geographic.* Several of Pesek's paintings can be found in the permanent collection of the Smithsonian Institution, as well as in private collections.

In the half-dozen years following his *National Geographic* work, Pesek has illustrated and written many books: *UFOs, The Ocean World, Journey to the Planets, Planet Earth* (all with text by Peter Ryan and published by Penguin Books), *Space Shuttles* (with Bruno Stanek), *Flight to the World of Tomorrow,* and the magnificent *Bildatlas des Sonnensytems* (with text by Stanek). The latter coffee-table-size volume (whose title in English is *Picture Atlas of the Solar System*) contains thirty-eight color paintings, the bulk of them full or double-page reproductions.  □

# LUDEK PESEK

Right, above: *Exploring a Martian "river channel."* Right, below: *The Martian south polar cap, covered with a mixture of carbon dioxide ("dry ice") and water. Both by Ludek Pesek (courtesy of the artist).*

*A moonquake in the lunar highlands has shaken loose a pair of boulders that have rolled down a slope—an event recorded by Lunar Orbiter photographs. By Ludek Pesek (courtesy of the artist).*

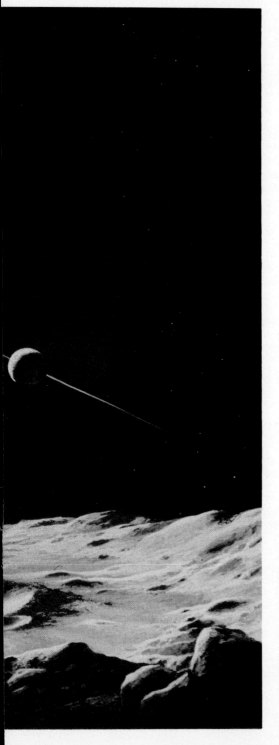

Above: *Uranus, as seen from Umbriel, with an inner moon, Ariel, above. This painting was executed before the discovery of the planet's rings. By Ludek Pesek (Starlog Magazine Collection, courtesy of the artist).*
Left: *Saturn fills the sky of Rhea, one of the moons closest to the giant planet, with an even nearer moon, Mimas, in the plane of the rings. The rings appear as a thin white line, as they would from most of Saturn's other moons. By Ludek Pesek (Von Del Chamberlain Collection).*

# LUCIEN RUDAUX

French astronomer Lucien Rudaux (1874-1947) was the first true astronomical artist. While many other artists had illustrated extraterrestrial scenes before him, Rudaux was the first to specialize in this subject and was the first to attempt to popularize astronomy equally through art and text. Over a period of nearly forty years, Rudaux wrote and illustrated many enormously successful books on astronomy, including the encyclopedic and authoritative *Astronomy* (Larousse, 1948).

As a colleague said of Rudaux following the latter's death: "With relatively simple methods, served by an inexhaustible ingenuity and an ardent love of astronomy, Rudaux made innumerable observations which very early made him familiar with all celestial phenomena. It is that which gave his works the touch of something alive, which made them so animated."

Rudaux's work benefitted from a unique combination of skills. He was not only a talented and skilled artist, but a professional astronomer of international standing. In 1894, he founded the Observatory of Donville (in the department of Manche, France), for which he also served as Director. The observatory specialized in observations of the Moon, planets, and the Milky Way. For his outstanding work in astronomy, Rudaux was made a knight of the Legion d'Honneur. He was a member of the Societe Astronomique de France, for which he served three terms as a council member; a member of the Comite National d'Astronomique; and a member of the prestigious l'Union Astronomique Internationale, among many other honors.

Rudaux's paintings and articles appeared in many popular publications of the day, including *La Nature, L'Illustration, The Illustrated London News* (where they were seen and admired by Chesley Bonestell, who still owns many of Rudaux's books) and even the *Annual Report of the Smithsonian Institution*. Reprints of his work also appeared in this country in magazines like *Popular Science*. His own books bore titles like *Comment d'etudier les Etoiles (How to Study the Stars); Sur les Autres Mondes (On Other Worlds)*, probably the first book of space art ever published—it contained over one hundred paintings, many in full color; and *Manuel Practique d'Astronomie (Practical Manual of Astronomy)*.

The artist used watercolor and tempera and painted in a loose, impressionistic style. His paintings are not burdened with extreme detail and are simple and geometric in design. They have a matter-of-factness about them that no other painter who had attempted space scenes had achieved. To Rudaux, he was not painting fantastic, imaginary worlds, but places as real and substantial as our own Earth. His technique, his belief and intimate knowledge of the reality of what he illustrated, and his mastery of perspective and lighting gave his art a realism never before achieved. Without trying to be photographic, his paintings have the appearance of being painted from life.

Rudaux's careful attention to scientific accuracy is especially evident in his paintings of the lunar surface. Unlike his predecessors and contemporaries (most notably Scriven Bolton, the Abbe Moreux, and even lunar expert James Nasmyth)—indeed, unlike most space artists until the present—Rudaux did not paint craggy, precipitous moonscapes. In fact, his depiction of the Moon's surface often bears an uncanny resemblance to Apollo photographs. This was due to the special knowledge afforded the professional astronomer. In *Astronomy* Rudaux pointed out that one can actually *see* the lunar mountains in profile by simply looking through a telescope at the edge of the Moon, silhouetted against the night sky.

Because of the authenticity and quality of his work, as well as its wide-spread publication, Rudaux was enormously influential during the infancy of astronomical art. He established a high standard for detail, accuracy, and aesthetics—an influence still felt today through the work of others he inspired. □

*Saturn, as seen from Rhea, from* Sur les Autres Mondes, *1937. By Lucien Rudaux.*

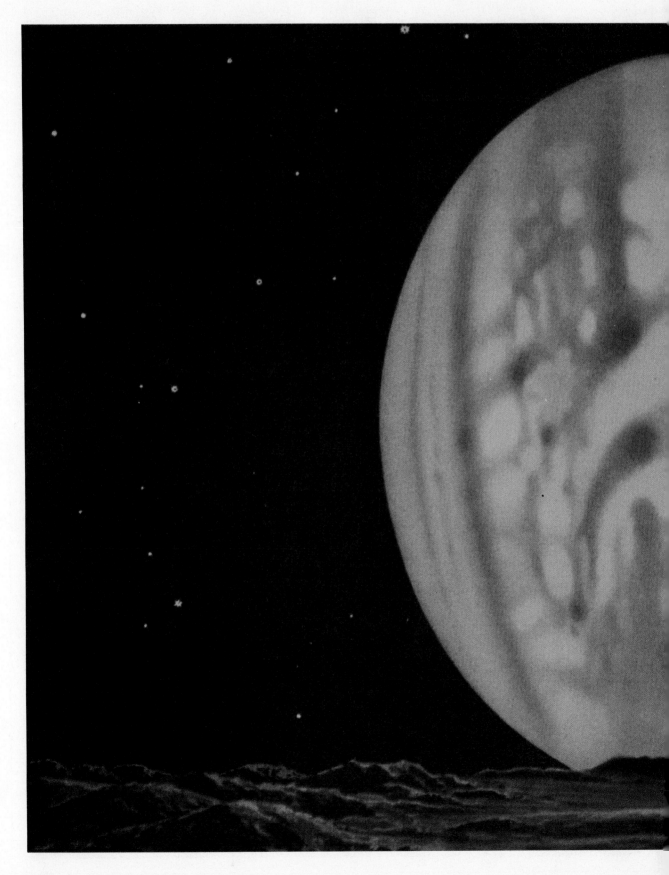

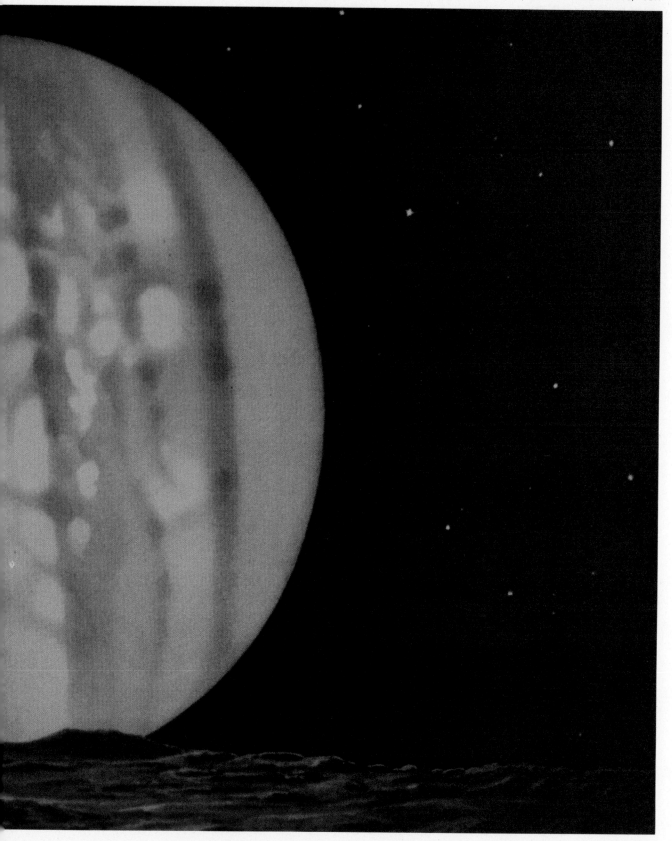

*Jupiter, as seen from its nearest large moon, Io. By Lucien Rudaux, from* Sur les Autres Mondes, *1937.*

Above: *A typical lunar landscape, from*
La Lune et son Histoire, *1947.*
Left: *The Milky Way galaxy, as visible during the long lunar*
*night, from* Sur les Autres Mondes, *1937. Both by Lucien Rudaux.*

# The Big Back Yard

The astronomical artist has always been aware that there are other worlds that are sometimes vastly larger and more substantial than our own. The bright, unblinking stars that drift across the night sky are planets that possess landscapes of their own: beautiful, terrifying, eerie, and, perhaps, even strangely familiar. The other planets that share the solar system with the Earth fascinate and propel the imagination of the space artist. The spate of interplanetary unmanned probes in the past decade have increased the artists' interest, just as the probes have served to raise further mysteries for the scientists.

Artists have served a vital function in the exploration of space. In the nineteenth century, artists accompanied the first expeditions into the Yellowstone and Yosemite regions. Famed landscape painter Thomas Moran accompanied the Hayden expedition that first explored Yellowstone. In addition to the scientific data, Moran's heroic canvases—and those of other artists that depicted the virgin, natural wonders of the regions—convinced Congress, and the tens of thousands who viewed them, to set aside this area as our first national park. The artists who tried to realistically portray the conditions on our sister worlds fulfilled the same function in the history of space exploration.

Here, then, is a sampling of those versions of our sister worlds in the Big Back Yard of the solar system. ☐

# MERCURY

*Mariner 10, on one of its historic fly-bys of Mercury in 1974 and 1975. The bright, rayed crater at lower left is Kuiper, and the irregular line above the spacecraft is Discovery Rupes, one of the giant scarps which meander across the Mercurian surface. By James Hervat (courtesy of the artist).*

*Sunrise on Mercury barely lights the distant peaks, allowing us to see the foreground landscape by the reflected sunlight. By Ludek Pesek (Ron Miller Collection, courtesy of the artist).*

*An imaginative interpretation of the surface of Mercury, with giant crystals growing beneath a massive Sun. By Sheila Rose (copyright Sheila Rose, courtesy of the artist).*

# VENUS

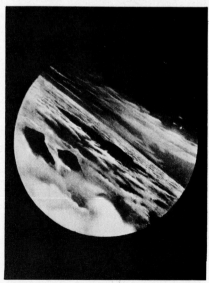

Above: *Venus' unpleasant surface, under an acid-laden sky (pressing down with a hundred tons per square foot), with an average surface temperature of 800°. By David Egge (courtesy of the artist).*
Left: *From a hovering spacecraft, only the highest of Venus' mountain peaks rise through the clouds. By Lucien Rudaux, from* Sur les Autres Mondes, *1937.*
Opposite page: *The dense atmosphere of Venus refracts light so much that the line of the horizon seems to curve up. By Don Dixon (courtesy of the artist).*

# EARTH

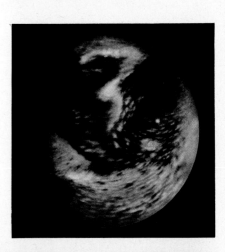

Right: *A pre-spaceflight conception of Earth, as seen from space. By William Palmstrom (copyright National Geographic Society).*
Below: *Looking east across the western U.S., as seen from Earth orbit, San Francisco Bay is in the foreground of this painting, created nearly 30 years ago. By Chesley Bonestell (Kerry O'Quinn Collection, courtesy of the artist).*
Opposite page: *Earth, as seen from its moon, painted in the late 1920s. By Howard Russell Butler (Smithsonian Institution Collection, courtesy of the artist's estate).*

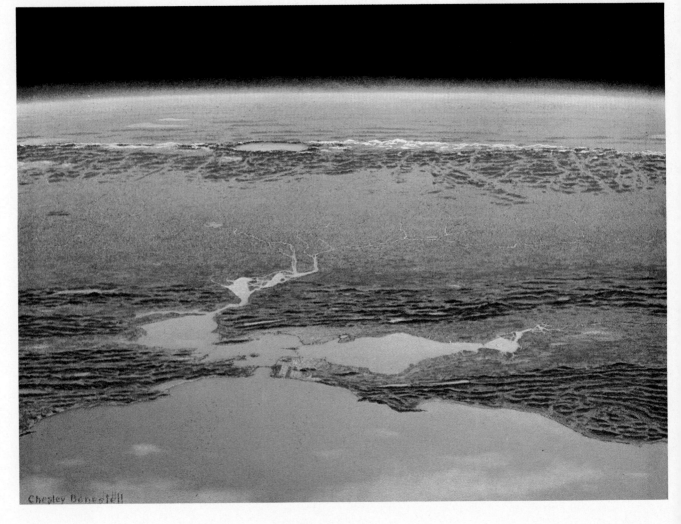

Chesley Bonestell

Above: *The shadow of the Moon crosses the Indian Ocean during a solar eclipse. By R. A. Smith, from* Exploration of the Moon, *1951.*
Right: *The Earth, as seen from different positions in space, including a polar view (bottom right). Created in the 1930s, these views were painted after consulting worldwide weather reports. By Lucien Rudaux, from* Astronomy, *1948.*
Left: *The Earth, as dawn swings across the Atlantic toward the east coast of the U.S. The artificial glimmer of major U.S. cities is seen on the far left. By Don Davis (courtesy of the artist).*

# THE MOON

Above: *The Earth is still surrounded by a disc of dust and debris "left over" from its creation, in this depiction of the "capture" of our Moon by the Earth's gravity. By Don Dixon (courtesy of the artist).*
Right: *The lunar landscape, bathed in the coppery glow of an eclipse of the Sun. By Chesley Bonestell (courtesy of the artist).*

*Millions of years ago, a small asteroid punched through the Moon's crust. The flood of upwelling lava cooled into the smooth plain known as Mare Imbrium. By Don Dixon (Starlog Collection, courtesy of the artist).*

Above: *A lunar mountain, Mt. Pico, as it would appear to an observer
on the Moon. By Lucien Rudaux, from* Astronomy, *1949.*
Opposite page, left: *A plaster model of the same Mt. Pico, made
in the 1880s from the same perspective as above, but illustrates the long-held
assumption that the lunar mountains are steep and craggy.*

Left: *A 40-foot mural of the Earthlit lunar surface, painted for the Boston Museum of Science, 1958, now in the collection of the Smithsonian Air and Space Museum. By Chesley Bonestell (courtesy of the artist).*
Below: *A manned rocket brakes down on the Moon. By Jack Coggins (Smithsonian Institution Collection).*

Top: *A lunar crater, lit by the light of a full Earth. By Mel Hunter.*
Above: *A typical lunar crater. By Lucien Rudaux, from* Sur les Autres Mondes, *1937.*
Right: *Earth, seen from the Moon, with the rising Sun lighting the distant mountains, while the remainder of the landscape is illuminated by "Earthshine." By William Hartmann (courtesy of the artist).*

# MARS

*A dust storm darkens the Martian sky. By Ludek Pesek (courtesy of the artist).*

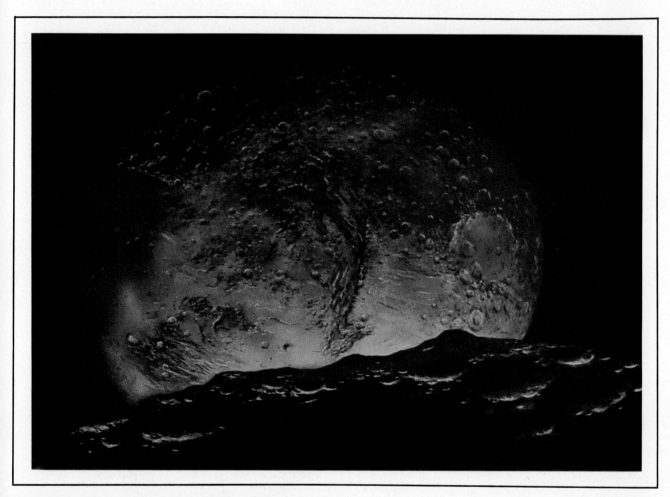

Above: *Mars, as seen from Deimos, the most distant of the two Martian moons. Deimos orbits so closely that Mars is only slightly more than 12,000 miles away, filling nearly a tenth of Deimos' sky. By Ludek Pesek (Ron Miller Collection, courtesy of the artist).*
Left: *Only a relatively thin layer of water ice and frozen carbon dioxide cover the Martian south polar cap. By Ron Miller.*

*The Viking 1 landing site on the Martian surface is depicted with meticulous accuracy, including the rock placements. By Don Davis (courtesy of the artist).*

Above: *Olympus Mons, the giant Martian volcano that is 310 miles across and 13 miles high, as seen from 60 miles above the planet's surface at a 25° angle. By Chesley Bonestell (courtesy of the artist).*
Left: *A Martian dust storm, as prophetically envisioned in 1937. By Lucien Rudaux, from Sur les Autres Mondes, 1937.*
Right: *A detailed portion of a painting that depicts the Viking 1 orbiting Mars. By James Hervat (courtesy of the artist).*

*Part of the vast Martian canyon system, Valles Marineris, with a ram-jet glider about to land. By Ron Miller (Star-log Magazine Collection).*

# JUPITER

Above: *Vista from one of Jupiter's moons, from the series, "Letters from the Planets" in* Cassell's Family Magazine, *1891. By Paul Hardy.*
Left: *Jupiter, as seen from Ganymede, with Europa and the speck of Io, two inner moons, on either side of the planet. By Chesley Bonestell (courtesy of the artist).*
Opposite page: *Jupiter, as seen from Io, as it eclipses the distant Sun. Io is one of Jupiter's strangest moons; it is surrounded by a glowing yellow cloud of sodium vapor and seems to be able to trigger violent discharges of energy by Jupiter. By Don Dixon (courtesy of artist).*

Overleaf: *A balloon-supported probe descends into the atmosphere of Jupiter. By Adolf Schaller* (Starlog *Collection, courtesy of the artist*).

Above: *Until a few decades ago, it was thought that Jupiter had a
violent surface of hydrogen-powered volcanoes with hydrogen ''lava''
and cliffs of frozen ammonia, as envisioned in this painting.
By Chesley Bonestell (courtesy of the artist).*
Left: *Jupiter, as seen from one of its moons.
Artist unknown, from* Splendour of the Heavens, *1927.*

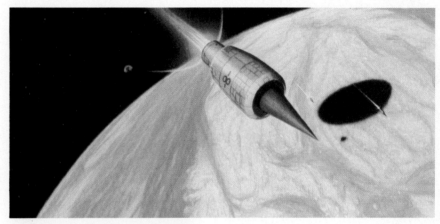

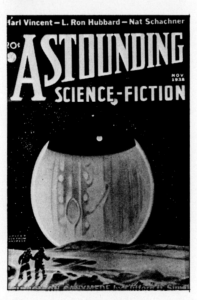

Above: *A ram-jet probe descends toward Jupiter. The small, red moon at left edge of the planet is Io, while the large, dark spot on Jupiter is the shadow of another moon. By David Egge (courtesy of the artist).*
Left: *Jupiter, as seen from Ganymede. By Howard V. Brown, from* Astounding, *1938.*
Far Left: *Jupiter, as seen from Io, one of the planet's four large "Galilean" moons, named for their discoverer, Galileo. By Ron Miller.*

# URANUS

Left: *An early theory of the nature of Uranus' rings was that they were composed of cometary bodies. This view looks down upon one of Uranus' poles. By Sally Bensusen (courtesy of the artist).*
Right: *Uranus, as seen from its moon, Umbriel. Also visible are two inner moons, Miranda and Ariel. The recently discovered rings of Uranus are among the darkest objects in the solar system and are unlike the brilliant ice-covered rings of Saturn. By Tom Miller (courtesy of the artist).*

# NEPTUNE

Neptune, as seen from Triton, the nearest of its two moons. Nereid, the outer moon, is only about 200 miles in diameter and orbits so far away from Neptune that the planet (which is over three times the size of Earth) appears to be the size of our Moon.
By Ludek Pesek
(courtesy of the artist).

# PLUTO

Pluto orbits in the comet-haunted darkness at the very limits of our solar system, nearly 40 times further from the Sun than the Earth. From that distance, the Sun is a brilliant point no larger than a star. Pluto's surface receives less than a thousandth of the solar energy that the Earth receives. By Don Dixon (courtesy of the artist).

Above: *Saturn, as seen from Rhea, one
of its smaller moons (1100 miles in
diameter). An inner moon, Mimas, is
seen to the right of the rings. Like
Rhea, Mimas orbits in the same plane
that the rings do, which is why the
rings look like a narrow white line
from nearly all of Saturn's moons. By
Ron Miller (Vincent DiFate Collection).
Opposite page: Saturn, as seen from its
nearest satellite, Mimas. By Abbe Moreaux.*

# Everybody's Favorite Planet

$\mathcal{S}$aturn has always held a special fascination for the space artist. With the possible exception of the Earth's Moon, Saturn has been the subject of more space art than any other celestial object. Certainly, the rings of Saturn are the most mystically awesome and lovely sights in the solar system. The rings have been represented in an endless variety of aspects and views.

Of all the representations of the Earth's Moon and neighbor planets in the last century, those of Saturn have always been remarkably accurate scientifically. Other than the depiction of the solid surface, the view of Saturn's rings in the 1877 illustration by P. Phillipoteaux for Verne's *Off On a Comet* is as accurate as those done by Rudaux and Bonestell nearly seventy-five years later. And today, the visual appeal of Saturn continues to lure painters to explore further views of everybody's favorite planet. ☐

# SATURN

Overleaf: *Saturn overwhelms the sky of its near moon, Mimas. The dark band at the midpoint of the planet is the shadow of the rings (the thin white line across the center, lit by the below-the-horizon Sun). By Ludek Pesek (courtesy of the artist).*

Above: *Exploring Tethys, one of Saturn's moons. Enceladus is seen in the plane of the rings. By Ron Miller.*
Left: *Saturn, as seen from Rhea. Four inner satellites are visible in the plane of the rings, as is the dark shadow band cast by the rings on the planet's surface. By Chesley Bonestell, from* Conquest of Space, *1949.*
Opposite page: *The Voyager spacecraft passes by Saturn by James Hervat (all, courtesy of the artists).*

Overleaf: *A view from within Saturn's rings, which are comprised of millions of individual moonlets of ice and ice-covered rock, each in its own orbit. By Ludek Pesek (Starlog Magazine Collection, courtesy of the artist).*

Left: *Hovering just above Saturn's rings, looking into the Sun as it is being eclipsed by the planet. The Sun's light, tinted reddish-orange by refraction through Saturn's atmosphere, lights the rings with a golden hue. Ice crystals in the rings create the halo.* By Don Davis (courtesy of the artist).

Opposite page, far left: *Saturn's rings, seen during a midsummer night from 40° N. latitude, looking south.* By Chesley Bonestell, from Conquest of Space, 1949.

Opposite page, middle: *The shadow of Saturn falls across the rings in this illustration.* By P. Phillipoteaux, from Off On a Comet, 1877.

Opposite page, right: *Saturn's rings at midnight during the summer solstice.* By Lucien Rudaux, from Sur les Autres Mondes, 1937.

Below, left: *Saturn and its rings.* By Alex Schomburg, from Science Fiction Plus, 1953.

Below: *About to intercept a ring-particle, a spacecraft passes through Cassini's Division, the dark ring between the two brightest of Saturn's rings.* By Lonny Buinis (courtesy of the artist).

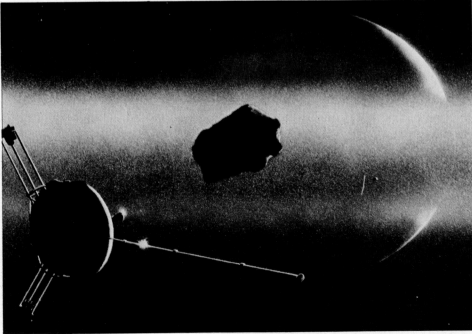

*Saturn, as seen from Iapetus, Although Iapetus is nearly 8 times further from Saturn than our Moon is from Earth, Saturn appears 4 times larger than the terrestrial Moon. Iapetus is one of the only moons in Saturn's system from which the rings appear open rather than as a thin line. Saturn's largest moon, Titan, is a small red dot between the two peaks on the left. By Ludek Pesek (courtesy of the artist).*

Above: *Saturn's largest moon, Titan, may be blanketed by a totally opaque orange cloud-cover, so that Saturn is rarely, if ever, visible. Titan's surface may be covered with organic molecular deposits that sift down from the clouds.* Methane geysers erupt volcanically. By Ron Miller. Right: *The "traditional" representation of Saturn, as seen from Titan, depicts the planet in a blue sky. By Ludek Pesek (Ron Miller Collection, courtesy of the artist).*

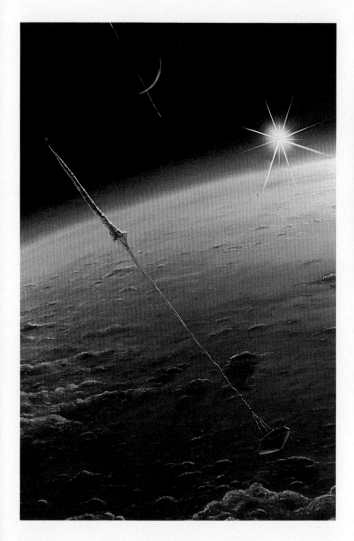

Above: *Saturn, as seen from the vicinity of Titan, which is not only the planet's largest satellite, but one of the largest moons in the solar system. Larger even than Mercury, Titan may hold an atmosphere as dense as the Earth's. By Don Dixon (courtesy of the artist).*
Left: *A probe, with its drogue chute unfurling, descends into the atmosphere of Titan. By James Hervat (courtesy of the artist).*

# COMETS, ETC. . . .

Above: *A comet lights the night sky of Mercury. Comets are largely composed of low-melting "ice" solids, such as water, methane, carbon dioxide, ammonia. As comets approach the Sun, these solids are heated and evaporated into dust and gas which is forced away from the Sun by the solar wind. The result is a streaming long "tail" of brilliant color which elongates the closer the comet approaches the Sun. Conversely, a comet's tail precedes the comet as the comet moves away from the Sun, again a result of the solar winds. By Ludek Pesek (David Morrison Collection, courtesy of the artist).*
Right: *A fireball, a meteor of unusual size and brilliance, streams above an English countryside. Artist unknown, from Splendour of the Heavens, 1927.*

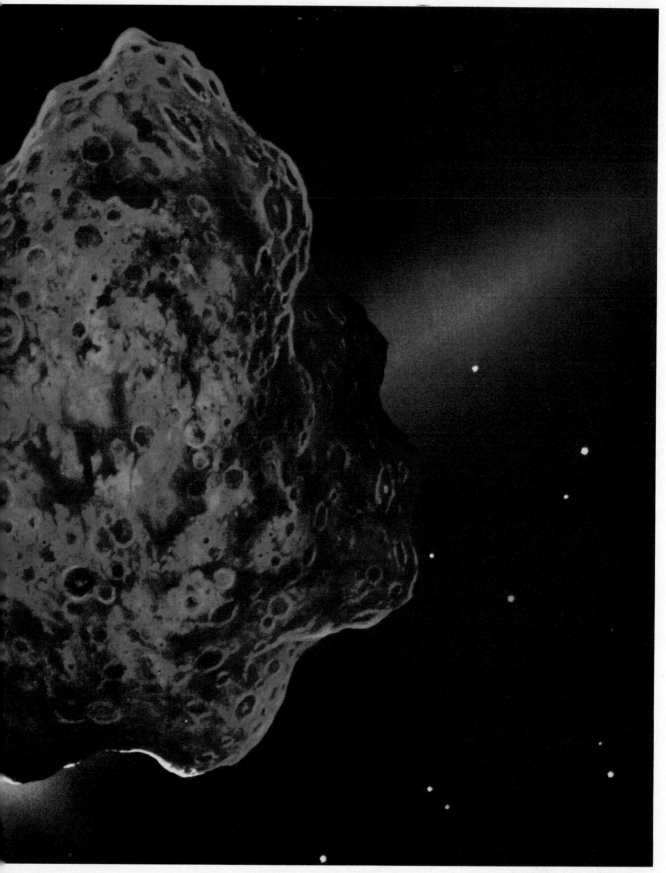

*The asteroid Icarus, as it passes by the Sun. Icarus, which measures about a mile in diameter, comes closer in its orbit to the Sun than Mercury does. Detail of a painting by David Hardy, from* New Challenge of the Stars, *1978 (courtesy of artist).*

Beyond our solar system, billions of stars move within the awesome spiral of our galaxy. Circling these stars are planets and moons and cosmic clouds of every imaginable size and color and composition. The celestial vistas are an inexhaustible source of subject matter for the space artist — an area of rich imagination and growing knowledge. And beyond the reaches of our galaxy, there are endless others . . . ☐

# The Galaxy and Its Worlds

*A spacecraft undergoes emergency repairs on a small planetoid near HDE 226868, a star in the constellation Cygnus. As the star plunges into a black hole, X-rays are emitted. By David Hardy, from* New Challenge of the Stars, *1978 (courtesy of the artist).*

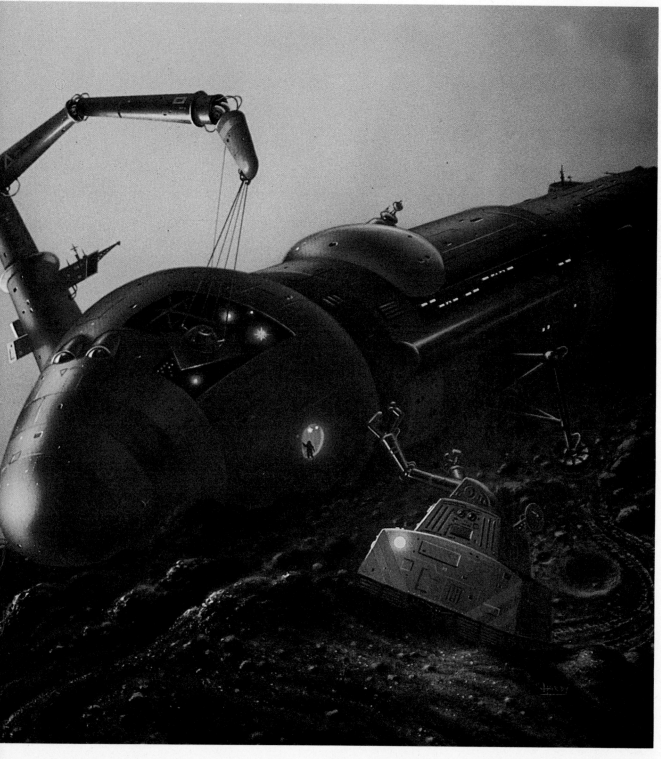

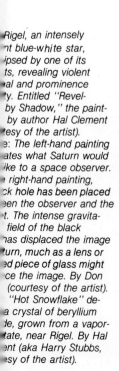

Rigel, an intensely
nt blue-white star,
ipsed by one of its
ts, revealing violent
al and prominence
ty. Entitled "Revel-
by Shadow," the paint-
by author Hal Clement
tesy of the artist).

e: The left-hand painting
ates what Saturn would
ike to a space observer.
e right-hand painting,
ck hole has been placed
een the observer and the
t. The intense gravita-
field of the black
has displaced the image
turn, much as a lens or
ed piece of glass might
ce the image. By Don
(courtesy of the artist).

"Hot Snowflake" de-
a crystal of beryllium
de, grown from a vapor-
tate, near Rigel. By Hal
ent (aka Harry Stubbs,
sy of the artist).

A hypothetical scene on an
inhabited planet that orbits
double star Mira Ceti (a white
dwarf circling a red giant).
By Ron Miller (Kerry O'Quinn
Collection).

Above: *The Milky Way is a double spiral that is 20,000 light-years in diameter and is composed of 200 billion stars. The core's pink tinge is due to the large number of older, red stars it contains.*
*By Don Davis (courtesy of the artist).*
Left: *The double-star system Beta Lyrae, as seen from an imaginary planet, orbits its common center every 12 days.*
*By Don Dixon (courtesy of the artist).*
Opposite page: *Earth is an alien planet to extraterrestrial visitors, and it may become a world alien even to ourselves one day.*
*By Alex Schomburg (courtesy of the artist).*

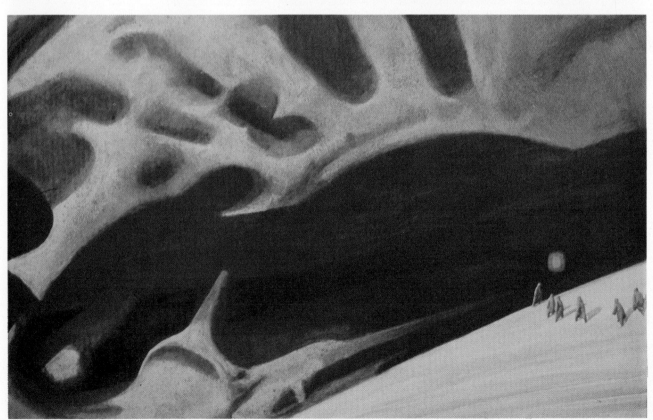

Right: *The double star
RW Persei, as viewed from
an imaginary planet.
Both stars share a common
envelope of luminous
gas. The smaller star
has developed a ring of
hydrogen. By Chesley
Bonestell (courtesy
of the artist).*
Below: *Exploring the
sandblasted surface of
a world of dust and wind.
By John Schoenherr
(courtesy of the artist).*
Opposite page: *The Milky
Way, as seen from the
Peruvian Andes, painted
while on an eclipse
expedition to South
America. By D. Owen
Stevens, from* Life, *1937.*

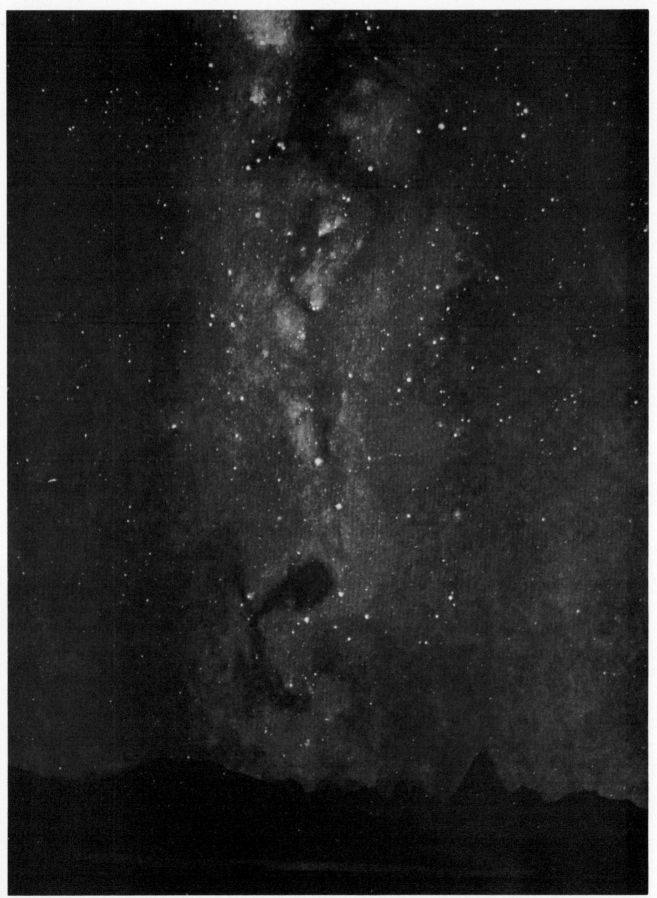

# How We'll Get There

In addition to paintings that visualize what we may discover when we explore space, there is a special sub-genre of space art that concentrates on the means we'll employ to do the exploring. These are the works of the artists who specialize in depicting spacecraft and associated hardware. Not all space artists have been able to successfully handle both subjects, because there is specialization even in space art. Notable exceptions are Chesley Bonestell, Don Davis, and Chris Foss; others, such as John Berkey or Pierre Mion are equally adept at hardware and figures.

There is a special anatomy to "hardware" just as there is to the human figure, or even landscapes. Rendering such hardware anatomy requires a certain degree of mechanical knowledge and a particular understanding of why machinery looks and operates the way it does—or why it might. Technical considerations are especially important when the machinery is being "invented" by the artist, since operational modes and structures must appear absolutely convincing while relating accurately to scientific fact.

No attempt will be made here to explore the hardware aspect of space art in depth, which could require a volume in itself. Still, the ramifications of space hardware art have been many, and its practitioners should not be slighted. The following examples spotlight the hardware artists. ☐

## The Hardware Artists

A modular space station concept, with solar panels extended to generate power for the complex's operation. By Denise Watt-Geiger (courtesy of the artist).

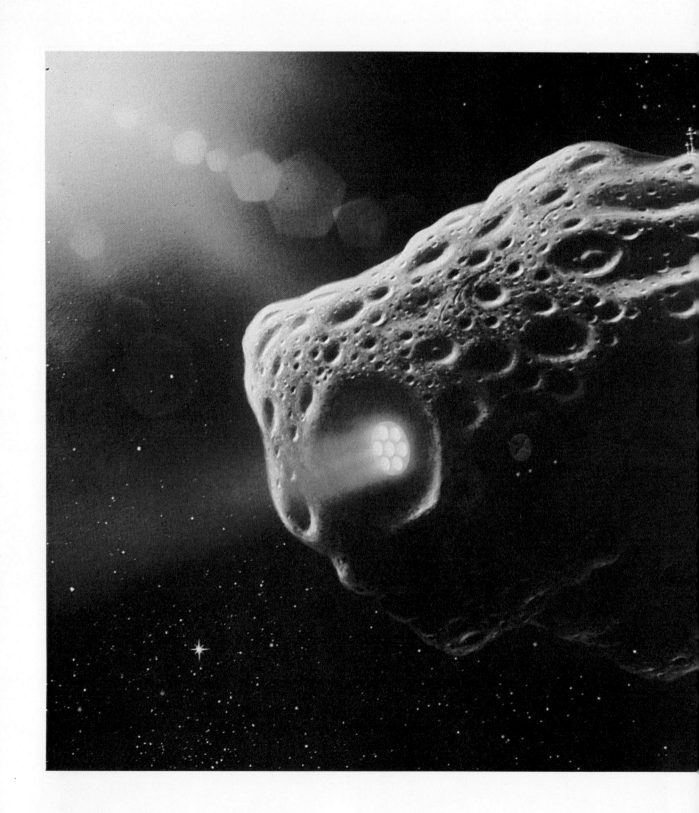

An asteroid that has been hollowed out to form a "space ark" which is self-propelled and self-supporting could be used for interstellar voyages. By David Hardy, from New Challenge of the Stars, 1978 (courtesy of the artist).

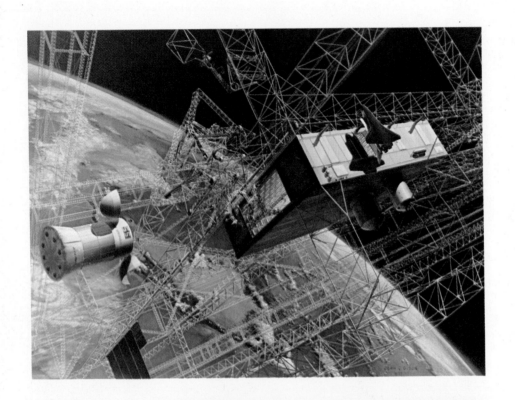

Left, top and bottom: *Under construction in orbit are two installations for generating power in space that will be beamed back to Earth. The top installation focuses sunlight onto a single thermal generator, while the bottom installation uses thousands of photovoltaic cells to convert sunlight into electriticy.*
*Top painting by Jay Mullins, courtesy of Boeing Aerospace Co.; bottom painting by John Olson, Smithsonian Institution Collecton, courtesy of Boeing Aerospace Co.*
Right: *The launch of a manned Soyuz spacecraft. Two original works by this painter are aboard the Salyut space station, which is therefore the first art gallery in space. By Andrei Sokolov (courtesy of Frederick C. Durant III and the artist).*

Above: *America's first Earth satellite, as envisioned several months before the fact. In addition to the satellite, an inflatable "Echo"-type sphere has been launched. By William Palmstrom (copyright, National Geographic Society).*
Left: *"Disaster at Syntron." By Syd Mead (courtesy of the artist).*

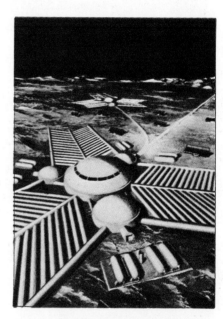

Above: A lunar colony, as envisioned
by the British Interplanetary Society.
These hydroponic farms are needed for
oxygen-producing capabilities, as well
as for food production. By R. A. Smith,
from Exploration of the Moon, 1951.
Left: A tanker-full of Titan's methane,
an excellent rocket fuel, crosses
the orbit of Saturn. By John
Clark (courtesy of the artist).

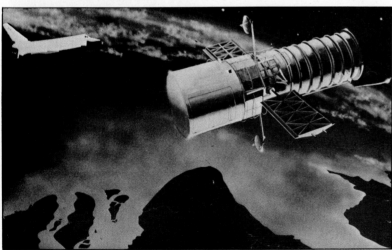

Left, top: *"A Pittsburg in Space" depicts
the mining of an asteroid for its
raw materials and possible metals. By
Chesley Bonestell (courtesy of the artist).*
Left, bottom: *A space shuttle approaches
an orbiting telescope. By Leroy
Williams (courtesy of the artist).*
Opposite page: *In this lunar colony, in-
habited structures are buried to provide
insulation and meteorite protection.
By Pierre Mion (Smithsonian Institution
Collection).*

Above: *A space suit, designed by the British Interplanetary Society in the 1940s. The astronaut maneuvers with a portable rocket device. By R. A. Smith, from* Exploration of the Moon, *1951.*
Right: *Building a space station. By Jack Coggins, from* Rockets, Jets, Guided Missiles and Space Ships, *1951.*
Opposite page: *Astronauts make their first Moon descent. By Fred Freeman, from* This Week *Magazine's serial, "First Men to the Moon," 1958. (courtesy of the artist).*

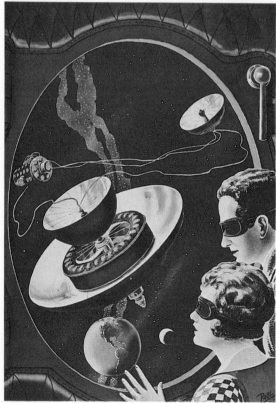

Above: *A futuristic wheel-shaped space station. By Vincent DiFate (courtesy of the artist).*
Left: *The first color painting of a space station ever published in the U.S. depicts Hermann Noordung's design of parabolic mirrors that provide power and a cylindrical observatory. By Frank R. Paul, from* Science Wonder Stories, 1929.
Opposite page: *Construction of a manned satellite in orbit 500 miles above Earth. By Chesley Bonestell (courtesy of the artist).*

Left: *Space station under construction. By
Jack Coggins, from* By Space Ship to the Moon, *1952.*
Below: *Construction of a wheel-shaped (toroidal)
space colony. The outer surface is covered with
panels made of crushed lunar rock that serves as
meteoroid and radiation protection. By Pierre
Mion (copyright, National Geographic Society).*
Opposite page: *A passenger rocket approaches a
Skylab-type space station. Observatory domes
are on both ends of the station, while a spherical
moonship is under construction on the underside. By
Jack Coggins, from* By Space Ship to the Moon, *1952.*

The concepts of space flight and astronomy have inspired a group of artists to explore not only the physical realities of the universe, but also what this exploration will mean to the human psyche. How will the opening of the cosmos expand our own consciousness? How will we reconcile our discoveries of the nature of the universe with our place in it?

The metaphysics of space exploration are as intriguing as the "hard core" sciences. Many artists have tried to discover what some of the human ramifications of space travel will be. Sometimes, these artists translate whole new emotions onto canvas; other times it is less anthropocentric. The artists usually attempt to discard some of our inherent Earth chauvinisms. New standards, new emotions, new meanings must be invented or discovered to translate and make relevant to humankind a set of conditions that is the *typical* environment of the universe—an environment alien and hostile, though indifferently so, since it may not yet be aware of Earth's existence.

These artists explore our universe in two directions simultaneously: to the illimitable worlds of curved space; to the infinite microcosms of our minds and imaginations. □

# The Universe and The Imagination

Left: *A mystical evocation of the almost hypnotic appeal of deep space. By Ray Crane (courtesy of the artist).*
Opposite page: *In the far distant future, the Sun dims and the Moon draws near during a frigid end of the Earth. By Mel Hunter (courtesy Time-Life Books).*

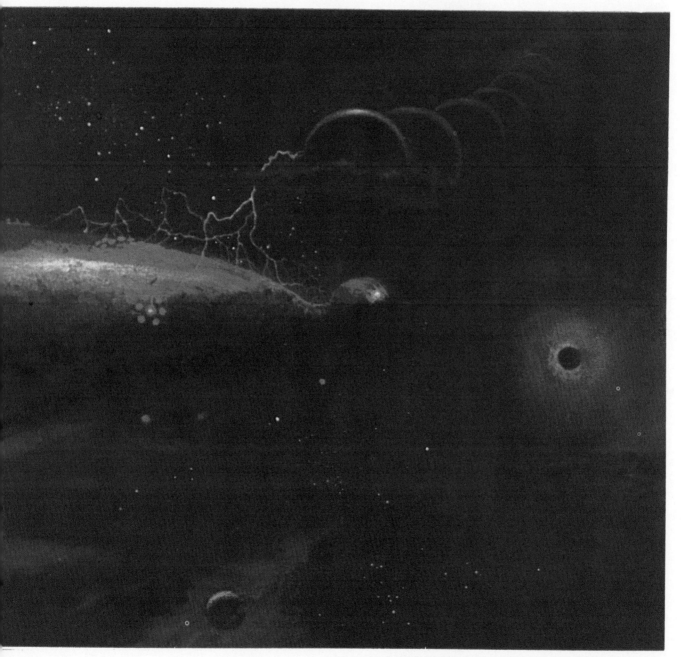

*A surrealistic evocation of spaceflight that combines elements of
hardware with organic forms. By Paul Lehr (courtesy of the artist).*

Above: *Technology may eventually fail, leaving us alone, faced with the unknown. By Mike Whelan (courtesy of the artist).*
Left: *"Cosmic Illusion." By Sheila Rose (courtesy of the artist and Pomegranate Publications).*
Opposite page: *Spaceship and landscape images, combined in a semi-abstract vision. By James Cunningham (courtesy of the artist).*

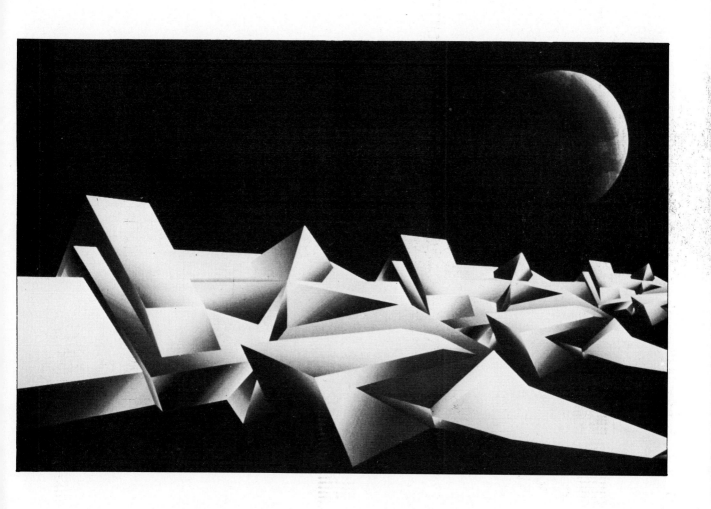

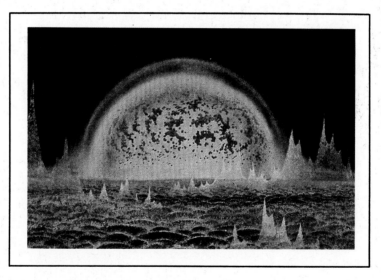

Above: *"The Boiling Planet," an alien world envisioned by a
Soviet space artist. By Andrei Sokolov (courtesy of
Frederick C. Durant, III and the artist).*
Left: *A graphic surrealistic depiction of gravitational
distortions of space time. By Helmut Wimmer (courtesy of the artist).*

# The NASA Fine Arts Program

Opposite page: "Sky Garden," one of the nearly 30 lithographs in the "Stoned Moon" series. Measuring 89"x42", this is one of the largest lithos in art history. By Robert Rauschenberg (Smithsonian Institution Collection).

In 1962 the National Aeronautics and Space Administration initiated the most ambitious art project sponsored by a government agency since the Depression when the Works Project Administration (WPA) provided work for more than 5,000 artists who produced more than 150,000 works of public art. With a sensitivity unusual for the government, NASA decided that, despite filmed documentation of all the agency's projects, there was a lack of emotional impact and significance to the recorded history. NASA concluded that artists should be invited to contribute their imaginations and perceptions to memorialize the agency's various programs.

In March, 1962, NASA administrator James E. Webb consulted David Finley, Director of the U.S. Fine Arts Commission (FAC), John Walker, Director of the National Gallery of Art, and Linton Wilson, Secretary of the FAC. Their recommendation was that NASA should retain Dr. Lester Cooke, Curator of Painting for the National Gallery, who remained principal art advisor to NASA until his death in 1973. James Dean, now Curator of Art at the National Air and Space Museum, was Director of the NASA art project from its beginning.

In announcing the inception of the program in 1963, Webb said, "Important events can be interpreted by artists to give a unique insight into significant aspects of our history-making advance into space. An artistic record of this nation's program of space exploration will have great value for future generations and may make a significant contribution to the history of American art."

That was a fine, inspiring statement of intent. But a more practical reason was that film and tape will not last indefinitely. In much less than a century, film becomes brittle, fades, or deteriorates. The materials of the artist, on the other hand, are potentially immortal. Many museum paintings and drawings are in excellent condition, although they are hundreds and even thousands of years old.

No aesthetic competition was intended between photographers and artists, however. In the words of Dr. Cooke, "These sketches . . . make it clear that the dispute between the photographer and the artist . . . proves nothing except that they are not competitors and do not tread on each other's toes. Both record a moment of truth, but on a different plane; and there is still no substitute for the artist's interpretation." In fact, it was not at all unusual to see the program's artists taking as many photographs as sketching drawings!

Fifty-three artists from the ranks of America's foremost painters and illustrators were included in the original NASA invitation. Not all of them took part in documenting any one space project, however. The budget was always small. The artists were offered little more than expenses and a small honorarium in return for their time and resultant art. Nevertheless, the response was almost totally affirmative.

One reason for this enthusiasm was

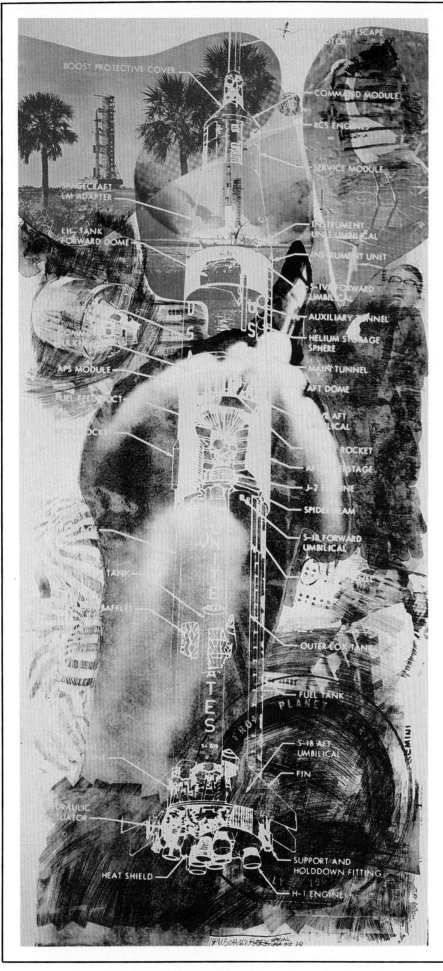

undoubtedly the passionately evocative letter of invitation written by Dr. Cooke, which said, in part:

"The efforts that we are making in this country represent the frontiers not only of technical achievements, but also of the imagination of the artists, and it is reasonable that artists should continue to be witnesses and recorders of our efforts in this field. . . . When a major launch takes place at Cape Kennedy, more than two hundred cameras record every split second of the activity. Every nut, bolt, and miniaturized electronic device is photographed from every angle. The artist can add very little to this in the way of factual record. But, as Daumier pointed out about a century ago, 'the camera sees everything and understands nothing.' It is the emotional impact, interpretation, and hidden significance of these events which lie within the scope of the artist's vision. An artist may depict what he thinks he sees, but the image has still gone through the catalyst of his imagination and has been transformed in the process. So style in this assignment is unimportant. If you see events in non-objective terms, represent them this way. NASA is commissioning your imagination and we want records of fleeting impressions and poetic by-products of thought as much as precise documents of optical experience. . . . His (the artist's) work . . . will become a permanent record of an individual's talent and perception, and in this way is a sliver of immortality."

Since the program began at the time of the last one-man Mercury launch, one of the first groups of artists naturally chose Cape Kennedy as their first assignment. To say that they

Above: "Blockhouse 34" at Kennedy Space Center. By James Wyeth. Right: If one of the Apollo missions had landed in the lunar crater Copernicus, the vista would have resembled "Man in Copernicus." By Francis J. Krasyk (both, Smithsonian Institution Collection).

© FRANCIS J. KRASYK 1969

were impressed would be an understatement, as one of the artists, Peter Hurd, bears witness:

"On the first night . . . Mercury Control Center was all but deserted and only a few lights burned. Moonlight ruled the stage, making pools of deep shadow from which emerged a long narrow scaffold of criss-crossed girders. This in turn was surmounted by a profusion of television antennae like fragile spangles of silver gleaming in lost-and-found pattern against the night sky. . . ."

The artists soon discovered that their sketchbooks provided excellent passports into virtually every area of the Cape.

The results of NASA's first "artistic expedition," were enthusiastically received by the press, critics, and the public who saw some seventy paintings and drawings at a National Gallery of Art exhibition, "Eyewitness to Space" (also the title of a book collection of NASA art, published by Abrams, now out of print). The space scientists and technicians, who at first regarded the artists with, at best, "amused tolerance" (as James Dean saw it),

Above: *Inside the Saturn 1-B blockhouse, technicians monitor the final minutes of countdown. The artist sketches while Wernher von Braun (in the dark suit at center) watches through a periscope. By Fred Freeman.* Opposite: *A blast deflector, as seen by moonlight. By John Willis (Smithsonian Institution Collection).*

later became increasingly respectful as they saw their hardware transformed into visions of fantasy and beauty.

That was the impressive and encouraging beginning. The fine arts program was enthusiastically continued through all of NASA's manned launches: the final Mercury flight, Gemini, Apollo, and Apollo-Soyuz. But, more recently, Skylab and the space shuttle have been given token treatment, because for all practical purposes, the program is inactive—due as much to lack of funds as lack of interest.

Was it all worth it? The program resulted in two major exhibitions at the National Gallery of Art in Washington and three exhibitions that travelled throughout the United States and Europe. Much of the art is now on permanent display at the National Air and Space Museum in Washington. Some of the artists, such as Lamar Dodd and Robert Rauschenberg, have gone far beyond their original commitments. Dodd has devoted more than ten years to independent development of the theme of man's relationship with the universe, which evolved from his original experiences with the space program. And Rauschenberg's famous "Stoned Moon Series"—twenty-nine hand-pulled prints, described as perhaps the most avant-garde lithographs produced in this era—was the result of his presence at the Apollo 11 launch.

James Dean urges the continuing need for artists to take part in the exploration of space: "...when explorers return to the Moon, as they surely will one day, artists must be among the first wave of new adventurers.... I hope that artists who have been involved with space exploration, or might be in the future, will continue to think about what they have seen and what it means. I hope that those whose philosophy of work permits, will explore mankind's relationship to technology, to flight in the air and in space and to our home in space—the planet Earth. I believe that in this imaginative visual exploration, we will see more clearly who and where we are and where we are going." □

Overleaf: *"Last Check" before an Apollo Saturn V Launch. By Henry C. Pitz (Smithsonian Institution Collection).*

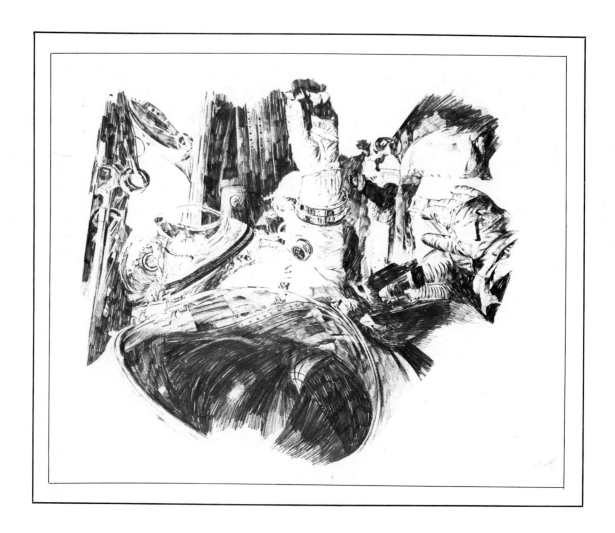

Top: *"To the Moon" lithograph. By John Meigs.*
Above: *"Ready for GT-4." By Paul Calle.*
Opposite: *"Gemini 7." By Paul Calle.*
*(All, Smithsonian Institution Collection)*

Overleaf: *John Young and Virgil Grissom before the first two-man orbital flight in 1965. By Norman Rockwell (Smithsonian Institution Collection).*

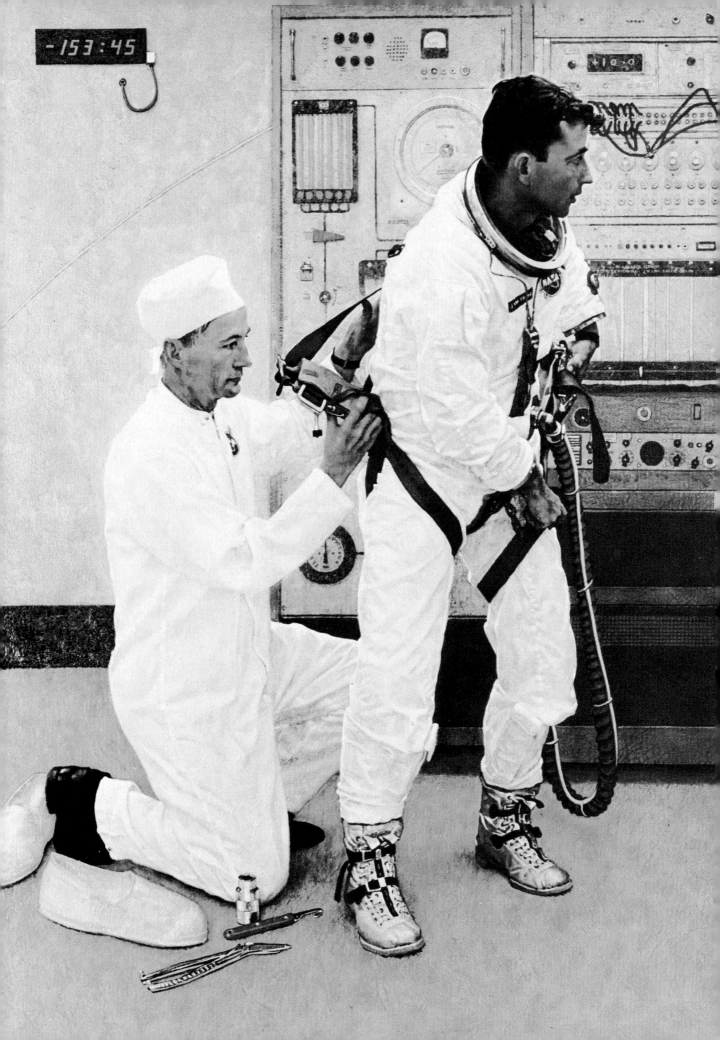

-153:45

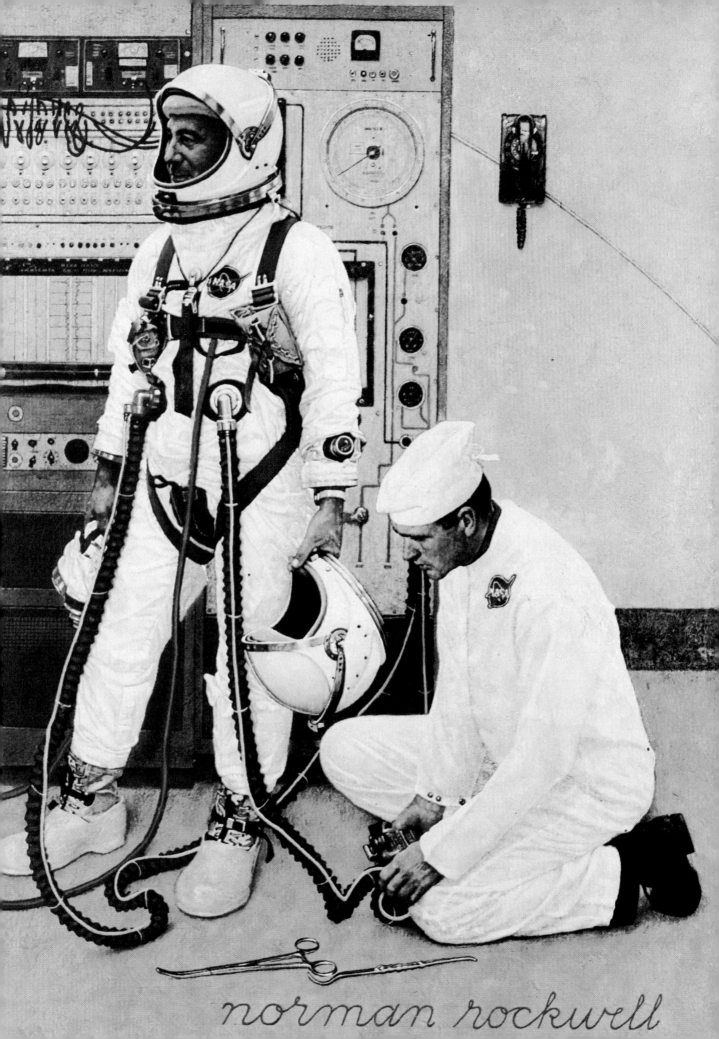

norman rockwell

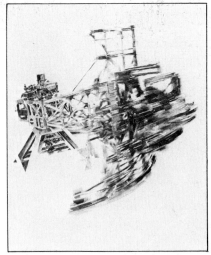

Top: *"The Start."* By George Weymouth.
Above, left: *"Interior View, VAB."* By Nicholas Solovioff.
Above, right: *"Centrifuge."* By Paul Calle.
Opposite page: *"Afterthoughts."* By Mitchell Jamieson.
*(All, Smithsonian Institution Collection)*

Above: *"Power to Go,"* the violent launch of a Saturn V rocket. By Paul Calle.
Opposite page: *"The Crawlerway from VAB."* The artist was the first painter to be allowed inside
the half-completed Vertical Assembly Building. By Paul Arlt (both, Smithsonian Institution Collection).

# The Great 1951 Space Program

During the early 1950s, when the world at large was totally Earthbound and worrying about the Cold War, sneaky Communists hiding in the closet, and the spectre of Korea, ethereal astronauts were already orbiting the Earth in a space station! Well, they weren't *really* up there, but according to the editorial staff at *Collier's* magazine, they *should* have been.

In the opinion of *Collier's*, the United States could indeed have had an artificial manned space station in orbit by 1963 and a fifty-man expedition to the Moon climbing craters by 1964. Today, glancing back at the magazine's embryonic space series and the trio of books it spawned, one is totally convinced that had the *Collier's* team of experts been given the mere $4 billion they said was required, they could have produced fleets of giant swept-ring spacecraft, launched a 250-foot-diameter space wheel, and assembled a mass lunar landing with ships filled with Caterpillar tractors and vacuum tube computers. And all this wasn't dreaming on the editorial staff's part, they insisted. The technology was *there*! "Speculations regarding future technical developments have been carefully avoided," the magazine stated proudly.

*Collier's* was a decidedly different magazine; one of the big four that flourished in the '40s and '50s; along with *Life, Look*, and *The Saturday Evening Post*. Unlike its peers, however, *Collier's* looked beneath the gloss of everyday life. It was famous for its exposures of corruption in national and municipal government. It printed quality fiction (some of Kurt Vonnegut's first stories found their way into its pages) and it often revealed tantalizing "scoops" of the latest military and scientific development. Perhaps, because of its unique approach to the world around it, *Collier's* was the first of the "big four" to die, disappearing in 1957, at the height of its popularity.

Before it vanished, however, the magazine succeeded in turning the eyes of the United States toward the heavens. During the course of their science-factual stories, the magazine managed to unearth advance information about the *Nautilus* submarine and other futuristic pieces of hardware. Eventually, they developed a few speculative pieces, such as one that tackled the possibility of launching atomic warheads from the Moon. Concern about the eventual military uses of outer space led the *Collier's* editors to investigate the feasibility of space travel in the (then) near future.

The entire *Collier's* space series had its beginning as a symposium on space travel held at the Hayden Planetarium in New York City in October, 1951. So impressed was managing editor Gordon Manning, that he decided to hold his own "symposium" of experts — a group dedicated to exploring the possibility of space travel in unprecedented detail. The resulting *Collier's* team included Wernher von Braun, then Technical Director of the Army Ordnance Guided Missiles Development Group; Fred L. Whipple, Chairman of the Department of Astronomy at Harvard University; Joseph Kaplan, Professor of Physics, UCLA (an authority on the upper atmosphere); Heinz Haber, U.S. Air Force Department of Space Medicine; and Willy Ley, authority on space travel and rocketry, who served as general advisor on the series. The group seldom met all at one gathering, but all were dedicated to making contributions. Oscar Schacter, Deputy Director of the U.N. Legal Department was consulted concerning the international legal aspects of space travel. The entire symposium and magazine series was put under the direction of *Collier's* associate editor, the late Cornelius Ryan. "Connie" Ryan was a correspondent with the 9th Air Force in World War II, later attached to General MacArthur's headquarters in Japan. He was present at the Bikini atomic bomb test and covered the war in Israel. Ryan later authored *The Longest Day* and *A Bridge Too Far*. To translate the concepts of von Braun and Ley into visual form, Ryan chose Chesley Bonestell, whose work had appeared several times before in *Collier's*; Fred Freeman, veteran *Collier's* illustrator; and Rolf Klep, technical artist.

During the two-year course of the series, a full-scale space program was outlined in the most minute possible detail. The first step would be the "baby satellite," an unmanned artificial Moon carrying three rhesus monkeys. It was to orbit at an altitude of 200 miles for sixty days before re-entering the atmosphere (the monkeys were to be given a dose of lethal gas immediately before re-entry). During this time, the thirty-foot cone would telemeter information on the animals' reactions and health, as well as TV coverage of terrestrial weather, which the authors predicted would be picked up by commercial broadcasters and transmitted nationally. The manned program would follow.

The series detailed the preliminaries to manned space flight: the extensive physical and psychological testing of the crews, the development of the space suits and tools, even the engineering of escape devices in the event of emergencies at high altitudes. The manned rockets were to be three-stage vehicles 265 feet tall (compared to the Saturn V's 363 feet), each with a crew of ten (the authors specified that women would be included) and a payload of thirty-six tons. The manned third stage had five rocket engines with a total thrust of 270 tons. All stages were recoverable, to be re-assembled later in a vertical assembly building, from which the rocket would be wheeled on a giant crawler to its launch site. It was suggested that the launch site be constructed at the Air Force Proving Grounds at Cocoa, Florida, near the present location of Kennedy Space Center.

A space station, 250 feet in diameter, with a crew of several hundred was to be next. A sign of the post-war times in which the series was created is indicated by the emphasis put on the station's military advantages. This was to have been accomplished by 1963 (1967 in a later estimate).

Nearby, a fleet of three moonships was to be constructed: two passenger ships that would eventually return to Earth orbit and a cargo ship that would remain on the Moon. An expedition force of fifty was to remain on the Moon for six weeks, travelling as far as 250 miles from base in peroxide-powered tractors. The expedition would leave unmanned monitors on the Moon to telemeter data to Earth continuously.

Later still, a manned expedition to Mars would be launched from the space station's orbit. This story inspired the George Pal film, *The Conquest of Space*.

The *Collier's* scenario prompted mixed reactions from readers and officials. The magazine's letters columns were filled with the enthusiastic responses of its readers, while, on the other hand, *Time* devoted its December 8, 1952, lead story to a less-than-salutory coverage of von Braun's ideas, as proposed in *Collier's*. *Time*'s editor refers to an "oversold public . . . happily mixing fact and fiction, apparently believes that space travel is just around the corner." Much of the article is devoted to von Braun's critics. Fritz Haber believed that the whole idea of space suits must be abandoned; Hubertus Strughold did not believe that men will be able to function at zero-g. And one of von Braun's bitterest critics said, "Look at this von Braun! He is the man who lost the war for Hitler . . . von Braun has always wanted to be the Columbus of space. He was thinking of space flight, not weapons, when he sold the V-2 to Hitler. He says so himself. He is still thinking of space flight, not weapons . . ."

The *Collier's* series on space travel was enormously influential, and continues to be. The magazines reached millions of readers, and the three spin-off books, *Across the Space Frontier, Conquest of the Moon*, and *The Exploration of Mars*, reached many thousands more. These books are still being read today. Countless scientists and technicians began their careers after seeing the series in their youth. The public was made aware of the practical possibility of space flight in their lifetimes. There was no more esoteric mystery about it—the knowledge, technology, materials, and money were all there. Following the *Collier's* articles, there was a surge of national interest in space exploration that lasted through the '50s. Every major magazine followed suit with their own speculations. Disney's *Disneyland* television program borrowed many of *Collier's* experts and produced a series of films that visualized, on TV, what the magazines did in print. It can hardly be a coincidence that only four years after the last of the *Collier's* articles, the U.S. launched its first Earth satellite. □

On the cover: *Chesley Bonestell's painting of the separation of the manned stage of a giant three-stage launch vehicle. From* Collier's, *March 22, 1952.*

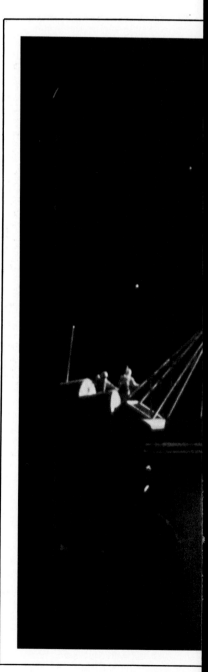

Above: *According to the Collier's "space program," the first trip to the Moon would be without landing. In this illustration, the ship is 50 miles above the Moon. The crater below the ship is Autolycus; the distant mountains are the Appenines. Detail of a painting by Chesley Bonestell.* Right: Collier's *later lunar expedition, 24 hours after landing. By Chesley Bonestell (Frederick I. Ordway III Collection, courtesy of the artist).*

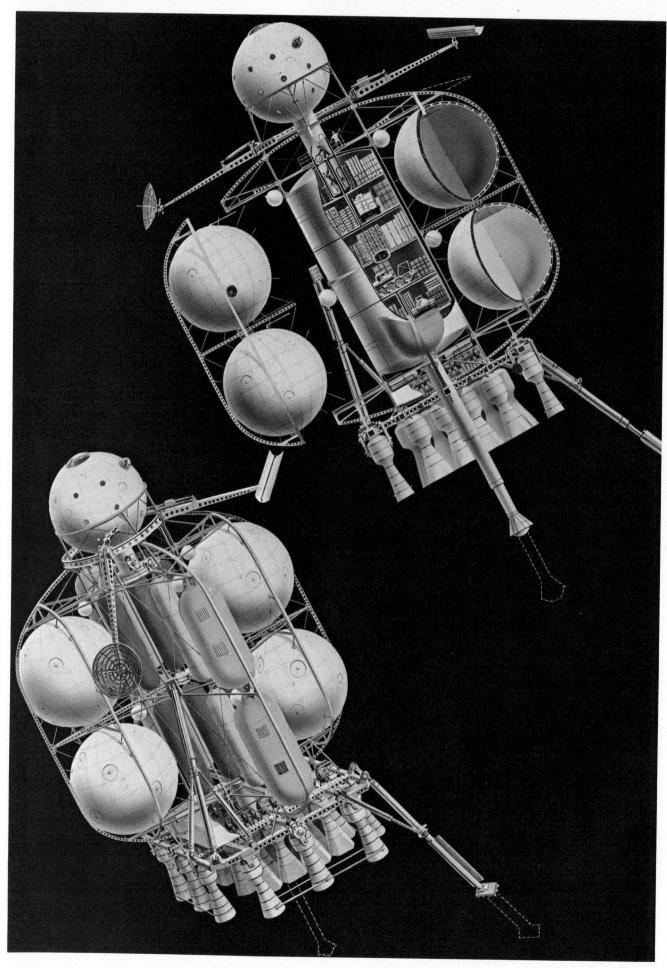

Left: *A moonship, at the instant of touchdown. The center landing leg, which will carry the weight of the ship at rest, has just been run out. Four outrigger legs keep the ship from toppling. By Chesley Bonestell (courtesy of the artist).*
Below: *Assembly of the lunar expedition ships in space, as they pass 1075 miles above the Hawaiian Islands. At left is the cargo ship. Other craft are passenger rockets. By Chesley Bonestell (courtesy of the artist).*
Opposite page: *The cargo ship (top) and the passenger ship. By Rolf Klep (courtesy of the artist).*

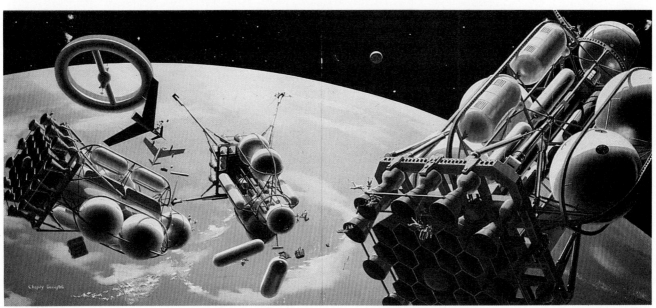

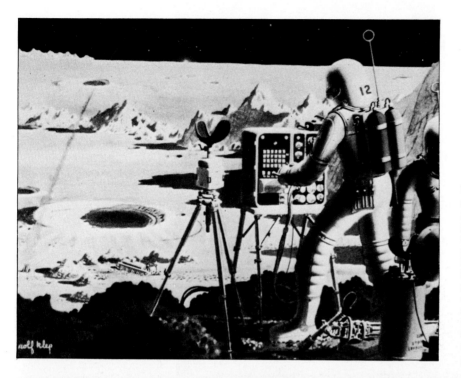

Left: *The Moon's interior is explored by examining the seismic waves created by "moonquake" rockets, detonating 50-pound explosive charges at distances up to 100 miles. By Rolf Klep (courtesy of the artist).*
Below: *The 250-foot space station designed by von Braun. It was to have a crew of 80, orbiting 250 miles above the Earth. Some of the main sections are (left to right): observation of terrestrial weather and landscape details, astronomical observation, elevator to central hub, life-support systems, and a solar mirror. By Fred Freeman (courtesy of the artist).*

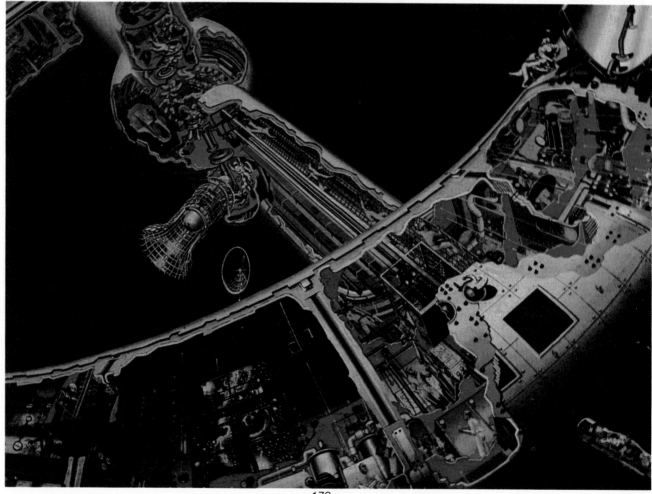

*Space suit designed for Collier's space series, with propulsion provided by a small portable rocket unit. The astronaut is tethered to the space station by a safety line. By Rolf Klep (courtesy of the artist).*

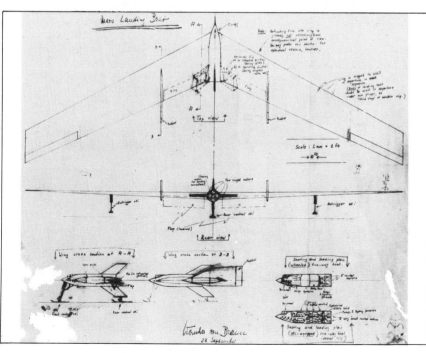

Above: *The arrival of the Collier's fleet of spacecraft in Mars orbit. The winged gliders are being assembled prior to their descent. The wingless craft will remain in orbit. By Chesley Bonestell (Adams Collection, courtesy of the artist).*
Left: *Wernher von Braun's own drawing of the original concept of the Mars glider (which he called the "landing boat"). (Fred Freeman Collection)*
Opposite page: *The three-stage passenger rocket, sitting on a movable platform. The 265-foot rocket develops 14,000 pounds of thrust from 51 hydrazine (green) and nitric acid (red) powered rocket engines. The top, winged stage would return from orbit like a glider. By Rolf Klep (courtesy of the artist).*

After the Mars gliders have landed, supplies and tractors are unloaded. The tractors have inflatable living and laboratory space above the driver's cockpit, and are driven by hydrogen peroxide engines. By Fred Freeman (courtesy of the artist).

# About Some of the Artists

## Jack Coggins

Jack Coggins was born in London and came to the United States while still a child. After studying at the Grand Central School of Art and the Art Students League in New York, he devoted most of his time to marine painting. During World War II he did many war illustrations for *Life* magazine, as well as many commercial clients. From 1943 until the end of the war he served as a U.S. Army correspondent in Europe. Then, in the 1950s, he executed covers for science-fiction magazines, notably *Galaxy* and *Fantasy and Science Fiction*.

In 1951 and 1952, Coggins collaborated with the late Fletcher Pratt on two classic books, *Rockets, Jets, Guided Missiles and Space Ships* and *By Space Ship to the Moon* (both published by Random House). The books were released amidst the great wave of national interest in space travel that swept the country in the 1950s. Like the *Collier's* magazine series on space travel, the two books made the prospect of space exploration seem a very practical possibility, and there are many space scientists today who retain fond memories of the influence these books had on their careers.

After illustrating Pratt's *All About Rockets and Jets* (Random House, 1955), Coggins wrote and illustrated books on military and naval history. He is on the Advisory Committee of the Philadelphia Maritime Museum and is a member of the National Defense Association and the U.S. Naval Institute. His original manuscripts and illustrations have been collected by the University of Mississippi for their permanent collection of outstanding authors and artists. His paintings are found in many public and private collections.

## Ray Crane

Studies in physics and philosophy were a prelude to Ray Crane's education at the School of the Boston Museum of Fine Arts. Crane's astronomical art can be seen during programs at the Charles Hayden Planetarium in Boston, where he is currently artist in residence.

## James Cunningham

James Cunningham's brilliant, abstract evocations of astronomy and spaceflight are avidly collected and can be seen in the Smithsonian Institution, the Indianapolis (Indiana) Museum of Art, Indiana Central University, and international exhibitions. At NASA's invitation, he has documented the Apollo-Soyuz, Viking 1 and 2, and Helios 2 launches, and observed the Viking Mars landing at the Jet Propulsion Laboratory in Pasadena. Cunningham teaches art through the National Endowment for the Arts.

# Don Davis

Don Davis has had the rare privilege and advantage to have studied under Chesley Bonestell. Davis' work has appeared in scores of publications, particularly in connection with his now-classic renderings of space-colony concepts. He recently provided a painting and sixty meticulous black-and-white drawings to a new edition of Gerard O'Neill's *The High Frontier*. He has also illustrated for science-fiction magazines. He worked for several years with the U.S. Geological Survey, providing paintings that illustrated the evolution of the lunar landscape, interpretations of the surface of Venus, and all phases of the Viking Mars mission. He provided the mural which backed the Jet Propulsion Laboratory's duplicate Viking lander. And his paintings have been reproduced on international postage stamps.

# Vincent DiFate

Vincent DiFate was born in Yonkers, New York, in 1945. He attended the New York-Phoenix School of Design on scholarship, winning over fourteen awards during that time. He has taught art and worked as a photo-engraver and as an assistant animator on the animated television series, *Spiderman*. Now a free-lance illustrator, he has worked for most of the major book publishers in the United States and Canada. He has also done educational filmstrips and several planetarium shows for the Andrus Space Transit Planetarium. He is active in promoting artists' rights, and is an authoritative lecturer and writer in the field of science-fiction illustration.

# Don Dixon

Don Dixon was born in 1951. He studied at Victor Valley College and the University of California at Berkeley, where he majored in mathematics, physics, and astronomy. He has been a free-lance illustrator since 1972. Thousands of slides of his space paintings have been purchased for use in educational institutions and by individual collectors. His paintings have appeared in many publications, including *Astronomy, Family Weekly, Starlog, Fantasy and Science Fiction,* and *Science Digest,* as well as in books like *Colonies in Space, Social Studies,* and *Astronomy: The Cosmic Journey.*

His art has contributed to several films, primarily through George Van Valkenburg Productions. Titles include: *Jupiter Odyssey, Probing the Clouds of Venus,* and *Good Neighbor Airlines,* all for NASA, and *Descent to Venus* for the National Air and Space Museum.

# David Egge

David Egge, born in 1958 in St. Paul, Minnesota, is one of the most talented of the young space artists. He began drawing at age seven and studied art in high school. He has concentrated on astronomical and science-fiction subjects almost exclusively for the last five years. His work in this area has won him numerous awards, and he has begun to make professional sales to publications and educational institutions. He is currently staff artist for the Foundation Institute.

# Fred Freeman

Fred Freeman, born in Boston in 1906, was christened by Edward Everett Hale, author of the science-fiction classic, *The Brick Moon* — an auspicious beginning for a future space illustrator! After many years as a commercial artist in New York — working in every technique and on every imaginable product, including the early airlines — Freeman volunteered for the U.S. Navy at the onset of World War II. It was not until the last two months of the war that he received an on-shore assignment as head of a thirty-artist unit preparing art for manuals and course-books. Here he met Theodore Roscoe, with whom he later did two classic books: *Destroyers in World War II* and *Submarines in World War II,* each with over a hundred illustrations.

After the war, Freeman's art appeared regularly in *The Saturday Evening Post, Esquire, Life, Look, This Week, Argosy,* and *Collier's.* His work for the latter magazine led to his being chosen as one of the three illustrators for the "Space Symposium." A portion of the material published in the magazine during the course of the series was gathered into two now-classic books: *Across the Space Frontier* and *The Conquest of the Moon.* Freeman worked very closely with Wernher von Braun, one of the major contributors to the series. Together, they produced two serial stories for *This Week:* "First Men to the Moon" and "A Trip to Mars." The first story was expanded and rewritten by von Braun and, with some ninety-six drawings and paintings by Freeman, was issued in book form. Freeman also provided the eight paintings and drawings for the *Reader's Digest* condensed book verison of Arthur C. Clarke's *A Fall of Moondust.*

Freeman was one of the artists invited to take part in the NASA fine arts program. One of the resultant paintings, a panoramic view of "Inside the Block House," is in the collection of the National Air and Space Museum where it is currently on display in the Flight and the Arts Gallery.

# David A. Hardy

Born in 1936 in Bourneville, Birmingham, England, David Hardy has nurtured an interest in science and art since his earliest schooldays. He illustrated his first book for astronomer Patrick Moore in 1954, and before that he did a series of large paintings for exhibition by the British Interplanetary Society, of which he is a Fellow.

He was asked to contribute to the making of *2001: A Space Odyssey* in 1965, but was unable to do so. He had his first one-man show at the London Planetarium, followed shortly thereafter by the publication of an enormously successful series of fine art prints. In 1972, Hardy and Moore collaborated on *Challenge of the Stars* (Rand McNally), which contained thirty-six full-color paintings. A revised edition, *The New Challenge of the Stars*, with eight new paintings, was issued in 1978. Recently, Hardy's artwork has been featured on the covers of *Fantasy and Science Fiction* and paperback book jackets. He has had many one-man shows. He lectures and writes articles and children's science books. He illustrates filmstrips and distributes slides of his art that are used internationally by educational institutions. His paintings are in many public and private collections, notably the Smithsonian Institution and the Marshall Space Flight Center.

# William K. Hartmann

Dr. William Hartmann is one of the three professional astronomers represented in this book who are also astronomical artists. Hartmann is Senior Scientist at the Planetary Science Institute in Tuscon, Arizona. His research has dealt with star and planet formation and the evolution of planet surfaces. He was a co-investigator on the Mariner 9 mission that first put mapping cameras in orbit around Mars in 1971, and he was a photoanalyst on an Air Force-sponsored study of UFOs in 1968.

# James Hervat

James Hervat's interest in space was inspired by the launch of Sputnik 1, when he was eight years old. Astronomical science fair projects won him local and state high school awards, and he has been a member of the Racine (Wisconsin) Astronomical Society since 1964. His main interests are in deep-sky photography and planetary photography. He has participated in two solar eclipse expeditions, one to North Africa.

Hervat's artwork consists almost entirely of portraiture and space art. He has had many one-man exhibitions and is represented in many collections, such as the Flandrau Planetarium and the Lunar and Planetary Laboratory. His work appears in *Sky and Telescope* and *Astronomy* and in a new textbook by astronomer-artist William K. Hartmann.

# Rolf Klep

A lieutenant commander in the U.S. Navy during WW II, Rolf Klep illustrated for many publications, including *Collier's, Life,* and *National Geographic.* He is now Director of the Columbia River Maritime Museum in Astoria, Oregon.

# Paul Lehr

Paul Lehr is a name long associated with science-fiction illustration, particularly paperback book jackets.

Lehr was born in 1930, received his BFA from Wittenberg University in 1951, and attended the Pratt Institute after graduation. His paintings are found in private collections in the U.S. and Europe and in museums, such as the New Jersey State Museum and the Smithsonian Institution. Aside from his science-fiction illustration, he has worked for many corporations, such as Westinghouse, GE, Pan Am, 20th Century Fox, NBC, and Time-Life.

# Tom Miller

Tom Miller is a graduate of the Columbus (Ohio) College of Art and Design. He has done illustrative and design work for the Center of Science and Industry in Columbus and for numerous publications. He also enjoys working in stained glass and is developing a series of fantasy and science-fiction subjects in this medium. He was an art director and illustrator for Larry Flynt Publications, and currently works at a studio in Delaware.

# Pierre Mion

Pierre Mion, born in 1931 in Bryn Mawr, Pennsylvania, has had a diverse career. In addition to his work as an illustrator for such notable publications as *National Geographic, Look, Smithsonian, Reader's Digest,* and *Popular Science,* he was a professional race driver for sixteen years.

For his illustrative work, Mion has worked with Jacques Cousteau and descended a South African diamond mine. He has documented several of the Apollo flights for *National Geographic* and was a member of the Apollo 16 recovery team aboard the *USS Ticonderoga.* He collaborated with Norman Rockwell on a series of space paintings for *Look.* His paintings of both space and non-space subjects have been widely exhibited and collected by such institutions as the National Air and Space Museum, National Gallery of Art, Smithsonian Museum of Natural History, Hayden Planetarium, National Geographic Society, Hudson River Museum, and the Society of Illustrators.

# The Abbe Theophile Moreux

Among the very small subgroup of astronomical artists who were also astronomers — a group that includes Lucien Rudaux and William Hartmann — was the Director of the Observatory of Bourges (Department of Cher, France), the Abbe Theophile Moreux (1867-1954). His work appeared in many publications around the turn of the century, the most outstanding being the encyclopedic *Splendour of the Heavens* (1927), and even authored a science-fiction novel.

# Sheila Rose

Born in 1941, Sheila Rose holds a BFA from the San Francisco Art Institute. She has had some two dozen major exhibitions of her work across the country and has appeared in many publications, most notably *Visions* (Pomegranate, 1977). Much of her work is also available in the form of art prints and greeting cards.

# Adolf Schaller

Adolf Schaller (born in 1956) is a wholly self-taught artist who lives in Illinois. He is one of the very rare artists to have mastered airbrush technique, particularly in its application to rendering natural objects. His work has appeared in magazines, as well as books. His film strips have been published by the National Geographic Society and Encyclopedia Britannica.

# John Schoenherr

John Schoenherr is, like Fred Freeman, a multi-talented artist. He is one of the finest and most highly regarded wildlife painters today. He has illustrated and written many children's books and has won numerous awards for them. Among those are citations for *Rascal, Wolfing,* and *Mississippi Possum.* At the invitation of the National Park Service, he has visited and painted the wildlife of most of the western national parks. He has been commissioned to do paintings for the National Speleological Society. Schoenherr has also been commissioned to paint for the U.S. Air Force. He attended the Apollo-Soyuz launch in Florida in 1975, painting and photographing the event. He is well known in science-fiction circles for his scores of paperback book jackets and *Analog* magazine covers. His illustrations for Frank Herbert's *Dune* series are as closely associated with the books as Tenniel's are with *Alice in Wonderland.*

He was born in New York City and studied at the Art Students League and the Pratt Institute.

# Alex Schomburg

Alex Schomburg is one of the genuine old-timers of space and science-fiction art. His career spans the very first Hugo Gernsback science-fiction and radio magazines of the 1920s to the present — his meticulous paintings still grace magazines and book covers. In over fifty years his artwork has lost none of its clarity, charm, or craftsmanship.

Schomburg was born to a German father and Spanish mother in Puerto Rico in 1905. The family moved to the United States in 1912, where he received a private art education. With his three brothers, Schomburg opened an advertising studio in New York in 1923. His first color magazine covers were done for Gernsback in 1925, for whom he continued to work until Gernsback's death in 1967. Schomburg illustrated for many SF magazines from the '40s through the '60s: *Amazing, Fantastic, Startling, Wonder; Galaxy, Future, Fantasy and Science Fiction* and many others carried his artwork. He illustrated the entire series of fifteen Winston Juvenile SF books, as well as covers for many Arthur C. Clarke books, and worked briefly on *2001: A Space Odyssey.*

# R. A. Smith

Ralph A. Smith (1905-1959) was one of the genuine pioneers of the hardware facet of space art. Smith was an early member of the British Interplanetary Society and was responsible for the visualization of the many spacecraft which that organization developed in the '40s and '50s. Like the late *Collier's* symposium in the United States, the BIS scenario for the exploration of space was the result of years-long planning by some of Britain's leading scientists, engineers, and astronomers. Although self-taught in engineering, engineering design ultimately became his profession.

Early work in architecture also stood Smith in good stead. His spacecraft were developed in minute detail. Indeed, if he were not convinced that an idea was feasible or practical, he would have no part in it. Before drawing any lunar background detail, he would carefully study photographs and maps. His paintings of the Earth from space were done with the aid of globes and high-altitude sounding-rocket photos — he is one of only two or three artists who accurately predicted what the Earth would look like from space.

The outstanding collection of his work is found in the book on which he collaborated with BIS President Arthur C. Clarke, *The Exploration of the Moon* (Temple Press, 1954).

Smith's paintings appeared in books, magazines, and articles all over the world and are now in the collection of the BIS.

# Andrei Sokolov

Russian artist Andrei Sokolov graduated from the Moscow Institute of Architecture in 1955. While working as an architect, he became fascinated by Ray Bradbury's *Farenheit 451,* which he began to interpret in paint. The launch of Sputnik 1 gave a further boost to his interest in space art. He eventually met Alexei Leonov, the cosmonaut and amateur artist, and the two have collaborated on more than fifty paintings which have been published in several picture books and in the form of postcards and commemorative postage stamps. During the Apollo-Soyuz Test Project, the art of Sokolov, Leonov, and several other Soviet artists toured the U.S. for six months. A painting by Sokolov of the Apollo-Soyuz link-up in orbit was used by NASA as the cover for their official report of the mission (NASA EP-109). The National Air and Space Museum has several of Sokolov's paintings in its space art collection.

# Denise Watt-Geiger

Denise Watt-Geiger attended Winston Churchill High School in San Antonio, Texas, where she won many awards for her work and ultimately a scholarship to the prestigious Art Students League in New York. She provided the March 1975 cover for *Amazing* just before returning to Texas. She soon found a position as an illustrator with a NASA contractor in Houston. Two paintings of a lunar colony, developed as a graduate thesis by architectural students John Dossey and Guillermo Trotti, are presently at the National Air and Space Museum. The three also collaborated for two years on the Rice University Space Station Study. Several of the paintings generated by this study have been published by NASA and *The New York Times*, and her art has been used on television by ABC and PBS. Two paintings were exhibited at the 1978 International Planetary Seminar. She has been working on NASA's solar-powered satellite program, while continuing free-lance artwork in the Houston area.

# Mike Whelan

Mike Whelan (born 1951) was introduced to science fiction by way of his father's collection of SF magazines and books.

Whelan eventually attended San Jose (California) State University, which he graduated with Great Distinction and as a President's Scholar. His original intention was to become a medical illustrator, for which he took anatomy and pre-med courses — a training that has stood him in good stead. After graduation, he attended the Art Center College of Design in Los Angeles. His first professional work appeared in the form of paperback cover art in 1974; since then nearly eighty paperbacks have carried his art. He has also done hardbound book jackets, movie posters, and magazine illustration — probably being best known for his "Little Fuzzy" paintings and for his covers for Anne McCaffrey's "Dragon" series. He is currently producing the definitive illustrations for Edgar Rice Burrough's "Barsoom" series and assembling a book of his work, to be published by Donning Publishers.

# Helmut Karl Wimmer

Helmut Karl Wimmer is the Art Supervisor of the American Museum-Hayden Planetarium. His works have appeared in many planetariums, museums, and scores of publications.

Wimmer was born in Munich, Germany, in 1925, and was apprenticed at the age of fourteen to train as a sculptor and architectural model maker. At eighteen he was in the army and served with the Alpine troops. At the end of World War II, Wimmer was captured by Czech partisans and turned over to the Russians as a prisoner of war.

In 1949, Wimmer was released and returned to Munich. There he found a job as a sculptor, restoring some of the damaged buildings. Among Munich's beautiful buildings in which one may see his work are the Theatinerkirche (in the Italian Baroque style) and the Michaelskirche (in Renaissance style).

In 1954, he decided to emigrate to the United States. Once in New York, a chance recommendation led him to an opening in the Art Department of the Hayden Planetarium.

Besides illustrating planetarium shows, his works have been seen in numerous publications, including *Natural History, Smithsonian, Reader's Digest, America, The New York Times*, and *Graphis*. He has also done occasional commercial illustrations, mostly of a technical nature. Best known are his paintings for a series of astronomy books for young people by Dr. Franklyn M. Branley, published by T. Y. Crowell. □

*Flight and the Arts Gallery at the Smithsonian Institution's National Air and Space Museum.*

Where
to See
Space
Art

Besides the collections listed below, there are several hundred planetariums in this country which have periodic space art exhibitions — works by their own artists, works on loan, or works they have collected. For specific information, contact your local planetarium or the planetarium in the city you may be visiting.

## Smithsonian Institution
Washington, D.C.
National Air and Space Museum
Flight and the Arts Gallery
The *major collection of art and graphics inspired by aviation and astronautics, includes space art by Bonestell, McCall, (including the original 2001 poster art and his giant mural), Rockwell, Pesek, Lehr, Mion, Calle, among many others, and the entire NASA fine arts program collection.*
Hirshhorn Museum and Sculpture Garden
*Robert Rauschenberg's "Stoned Moon" series of lithographs.*

## Hayden Planetarium
New York, New York
*Includes walk-through black-light space murals.*

## Adler Planetarium
Chicago, Illinois
Gallery of Astronomical Art
*Major collection of art by Chesley Bonestell.*

## Alabama Space and Rocket Center
Huntsville, Alabama
*Large collection of art by Chesley Bonestell.*

## Flandrau Planetarium
Tucson, Arizona
*Collection includes art by Schaller, Hartmann, and a mural by Bonestell.*

## Boston Museum of Science
Boston, Massachusetts
*Large mural by Chesley Bonestell.*

## Griffith Observatory
Los Angeles, California
*Paintings by Chesley Bonestell.*

## Broadway National Bank
San Antonio, Texas
*Large painting by Bob McCall.*

## First National Bank of Arizona
Tucson, Arizona
*Painting by Bob McCall.*

## NASA Headquarters
Washington, D.C.
*Art commissioned for NASA publications displayed in corridors. Art is also displayed at these other NASA facilities: Langley Research Center, Langley, Maryland; Johnson Space Center, Houston, Texas; Marshall Space Flight Center, Huntsville, Alabama.*

## Gallery Rebecca Cooper
Washington, D.C.
*Paintings by Sheila Rose.*

*Science-fiction conventions are excellent places to view and to purchase space art.*

# Where to Buy Space Art

Most science-fiction conventions have large art shows (usually, the larger the convention, the larger the art show). These are held all over the country during the year. Lists of forthcoming conventions, with addresses where information about them can be obtained, can be found in many science-fiction magazines, such as *Starlog, Analog,* and *Isaac Asimov's Science Fiction Magazine.* At the convention art shows, amateur and professional artists display and sell original paintings and drawings, normally by auction.

## Astro Art
99 Southam Rd.
Hall Green, Birmingham
B28 OAB, England
*Prints and slides by David Hardy (send an International Reply Coupon for current list)*

## Astro Associates
PO Box 9912
Chevy Chase, Maryland 20015
*Color prints of art by Ludek Pesek; postcards of art by Andre Sokolov; and* Eyewitness to Space *book*

## Astronomical Art
PO Box 274
Woodbridge, Virginia 22194
*Prints and original paintings by Ron Miller; original art by Ludek Pesek*

## Astronomical Art
PO Box 692, Gateway Station
Culver City, California 90230
*Slides and original art by Morris Scott Dollens*

## Bonestell Space Art
PO Box 36
Palo Alto, California 94302
*Prints and original paintings by Chesley Bonestell*

## Dixon Spacescapes
PO Box 723
Rialto, California 92376
*Slides and original art by Don Dixon*

## Donald Art Company, Inc.
230 Fifth Avenue.
New York, New York 10001
*Prints by Chesley Bonestell (Wholesale only)*

## Dream Masters
6399 Wilshire Blvd.
Los Angeles, California 90048
*A gallery of fantasy and science fiction art.*

## Flandrau Planetarium
University of Arizona
Tucson, Arizona 85724
*Prints and slides of art by Schaller, Hartmann, and others*

## James Hervat
PO Box 352
Kenosha, Wisconsin 53140
*Prints and original paintings by James Hervat*

## Peterprints
PO Box 1705
San Francisco, California 94101
*Color cards of art by Geoffrey Chandler and Morris Scott Dollens*

## Pomegranate Publications
PO Box 748
Corte Madera, California 94925
*Prints and cards of art by Sheila Rose*

## Portal Publications
21 Tamal Vista Blvd.
Corte Madera, California 94925
*Prints of paintings by Mead, DiFate, Berkey, Ellis, Sternbach, and Miller*

## Smithsonian Institution
National Air and Space Museum
Washington, D.C. 20560
*Museum Shop and Spacearium Shop Prints and reproductions of space and NASA art*

# The Making of a Space Painting

As in any specialized artform, astronomical art makes certain requirements of the artist who practices it. The space artist must be able to handle a representational painting technique. This does not mean that his painting must look like a photograph. Bonestell, of course, paints this way — partly a result of his experience as a motion picture matte painter, where his paintings had to fit undetected into the scene being filmed. Indeed, some of his most photographic paintings are in fact photographs . . . at least in part. A technique Bonestell practiced often in his earlier work was to construct a model of plaster, plasticine, and clay, photograph it with a pinhole camera (for maximum depth-of-field and clarity), mount a black-and-white print on a stiff support, and paint directly onto the photograph. His first published art was described as "photomontage paintings."

But it is not an absolute necessity for space art to be photographic in appearance. The real test is "believability," and photographic realism is only one way to achieve it. Ludek Pesek employs an impressionistic style, yet his paintings are quite realistic. They have all the appearance of having been painted from "life." This is because, to achieve believability, Pesek makes the landscapes in his paintings very natural: they do not seem to have been invented by the artist; they bear no marks of artificiality. If the viewer can be made to accept at least some of the painting as real, then he is forced to at least consider the remainder as representing something within the realm of reality.

Too often, what is shown in the skies of space paintings is strange enough to the viewer — the artist should not have such an unbelievable landscape that the viewer dismisses the whole thing as outright fantasy. There must be something in the painting for the viewer to accept as familiar. This is easy enough in paintings representing the planets of our solar system: there is scarcely any kind of terrain that is not duplicated in some way, or has its analogue, on Earth. Even on the outre, but scientifically plausible worlds of Hal Clement, rocks are rocks, clouds are clouds, liquids are liquids.

The potential astronomical artist must also have a diverse knowledge of the sciences, particularly geology, meteorology, physics, astronomy — most of the Earth sciences in fact. He will quickly find that little of the information available will have been designed with the artist in mind. He will discover that scientists seldom give any thought as to what their research means in terms of their translation by human senses. During the course of researching a painting of the Milky Way, I asked one of the world's leading authorities on our galaxy what it would look like if seen from "outside." His answer was, "I've never thought of that!" In a great many instances, the artist himself will have to translate what abstract scientific information means in visual terms. This is the value of the astronomical artist, serving much the same function as the paleontological artist (the only science other than astronomy to have bred its own artform) when the latter reconstructs some antediluvian monster. It is the artist who is bringing reality to what are otherwise virtual abstractions.

A thorough knowledge of perspective is essential. The artist is working with things that are *big*, vast, distant, and three-dimensional — and they should look that way. (To say nothing of the more bizarre problems, like how do Saturn's rings appear when seen looking east from 40° n. latitude?) The artist who wishes to include spacecraft or who wants to specialize in spacecraft alone needs an even greater knowledge of perspective. [There are several excellent books on the art of perspective, probably the most comprehensive being *Perspective*, by Rex Vicat Cole, recently reprinted by Dover Books, NY.]

A related necessity is to know how big, or small, a planet will appear in the sky of one of its moons. The Earth's moon appears to cover ½° of arc in our sky. That is, if a line were drawn from horizon to horizon, passing directly overhead, it would be measuring half of a full circle, or 180° — the Moon would cover, or "subtend", just ½° on this line. (This is, by coincidence, the same angle covered by the Sun, which allows us to have total solar eclipses.) This information tells the artist how large to make an object in his painting. For example, the usual "visual angle" for a painting (the amount of horizon included within a picture, out of a possible 360°) is about 40°, about the same field of view as a typical snapshot. Human eyes take in about 120°. Jupiter seen from its moon, Io, fills nearly 20° — forty times larger than a full moon on Earth, even though the distances involved are about the same. This means, then, that Jupiter would take up one-half the width of the painting.

Of course, strict scientific accuracy is not the ultimate goal or criteria of astronomical art. It should certainly be there, of course, just as good anatomy is necessary to a successful figure drawing. But as slavish attention to musculature and bones makes a figure drawing little more than a diagram in an anatomy text, astronomical art, too, needs more than its science to be valid. ☐

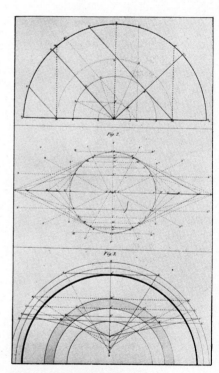

*The complex geometry involved in calculating the perspective of Saturn's rings, as seen from the planet's surface. From* Saturn and Its System, *1865.*

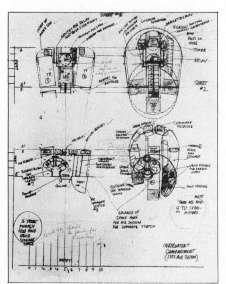

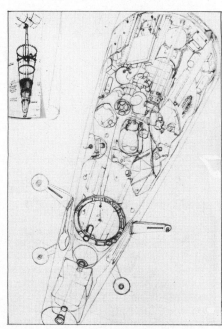

Three stages in the creation of a "hardware" painting. Below: Wernher von Braun's drawing of the original concept of the Collier's proposed "baby satellite." Far left: Fred Freeman's sketch of the satellite's interior works, with notes by von Braun. Near left: Freeman's detailed final preliminary sketch. Opposite page: The final painting of the "baby satellite," ready to be printed in Collier's. By Fred Freeman

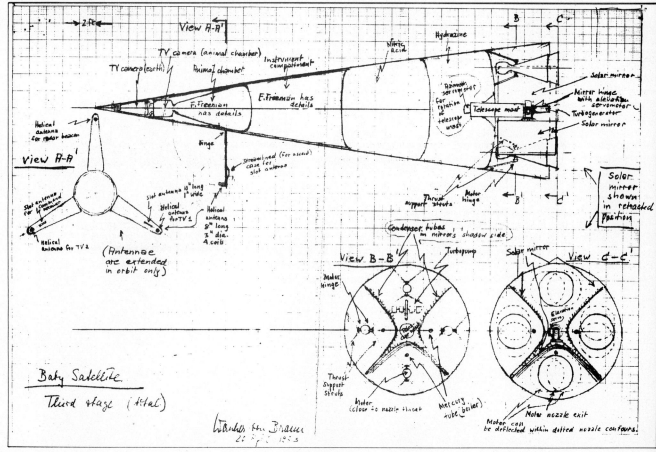

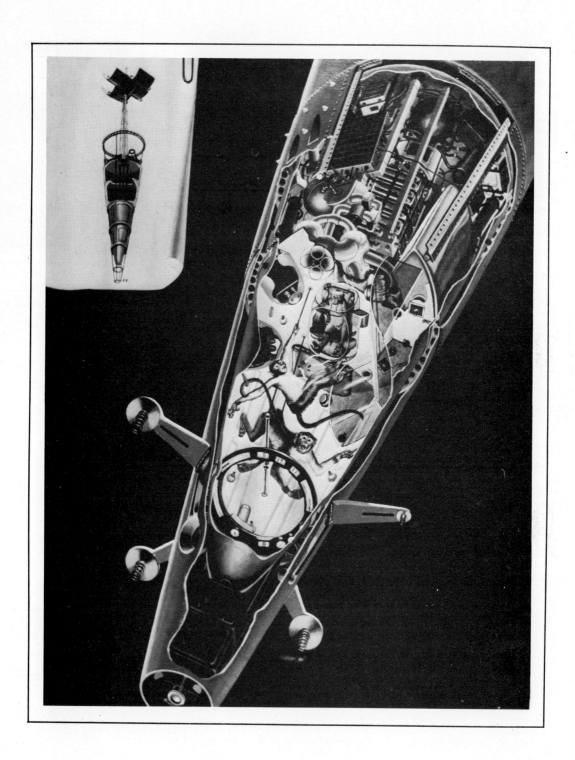

# Selected Bibliography

The Conquest of Space
*text by Willy Ley, art by Chesley Bonestell*
*Viking Press, 1949*

Across the Space Frontier
*text by Wernher von Braun, Willy Ley, and*
*others, art by Chesley Bonestell, Rolf Klep,*
*and Fred Freeman*
*Viking Press, 1952*

Conquest of the Moon
*text by Wernher von Braun, Fred Whipple, and*
*Willy Ley, art by Chesley Bonestell, Rolf Klep,*
*and Fred Freeman*
*Viking Press, 1952*

The Exploration of Mars
*text by Willy Ley and Wernher von Braun,*
*art by Chesley Bonestell*
*Viking Press, 1956*

Beyond the Solar System
*text by Willy Ley, art by Chesley Bonestell*
*Viking Press, 1964*

Beyond Jupiter
*text by Arthur C. Clarke,*
*art by Chesley Bonestell*
*Little, Brown & Co., 1972*

The Moon and the Planets
*text by J. Sadil, art by Ludek Pesek*
*Paul Hamlyn, 1964*

Our Planet Earth
*text by J. Sadil, art by Ludek Pesek*
*Paul Hamlyn, 1968*

Journey to the Planets
*text by Peter Ryan, art by Ludek Pesek*
*Penguin Books, 1972*

Planet Earth
*text by Peter Ryan, art by Ludek Pesek*
*Penguin Books, 1972*

Bildatlas des Sonnensystems
*text by Bruno Stanek, art by Ludek Pesek*
*Hallwag, 1974*

Challenge of the Stars
*text by Patrick Moore, art by David Hardy*
*Rand McNally, 1972*

New Challenge of the Stars (revision of above
work)
*Rand McNally, 1978*
*Mitchell Beazley Ltd., 1978*

By Space Ship to the Moon
*text by Fletcher Pratt, art by Jack Coggins*
*Random House, 1952*

Sur les Autres Mondes
*text and art by Lucien Rudaux*
*Librairie Larousse, 1937*

Our World in Space
*text by Isaac Asimov, art by Bob McCall*
*New York Graphic Society, 1974*

Eyewitness to Space
*art by NASA Fine Arts Program artists*
*Harry Abrams, Inc. 1970*

U.F.O.s
*text by Peter Ryan, art by Ludek Pesek*
*Penguin Books, 1974*

Solar System
*text by Peter Ryan, art by Ludek Pesek*
*Penguin Books, 1978*

# Acknowledgements

I owe a deep debt of gratitude to the many artists who so generously gave their time and works to this book. My only regret is being able to use only a slight fraction of the artwork available to me. Special thanks are due to Vincent DiFate, Sally Bensusen, Morris Scott Dollens, Kate and Fred Freeman, Rolf Klep, and Hulda and Chesley Bonestell. I greatly appreciate the kind assistance given by William C. Estler; Ron Gallant; Frederick C. Durant III, Assistant Director, Astronautics, National Air and Space Museum; James Dean, Curator of Art, National Air and Space Museum; Catherine Scott, librarian, National Air and Space Museum; Brenda Corbin, librarian, U.S. Naval Observatory; Howard Paine and Merrill Clift, National Geographic Society; Dennis Mammana, Staff Astronomer, Flandrau Planetarium; the editorial staff of STARLOG and FUTURE for their almost infinite patience; and my muse and keeper, Judith.
—R·M. □

# About The Author
## Ron Miller

Ron Miller, born in 1947 in Minneapolis, Minnesota, holds a BFA from the Columbus (Ohio) College of Art and Design. He worked for over six years as a commercial artist and designer — on projects ranging from package design, wallpaper design, annual reports, and newspaper ads to posters, magazine layout, and architectural rendering. He developed a life-long interest in space sciences into the hobby of creating astronomical art. This eventually led to a position at the Smithsonian Institution's National Air & Space Museum as illustrator/art director for the Experimentarium, a small planetarium built to develop techniques for the larger facility which was to be part of the new museum building. For the new planetarium, the Albert Einstein Spacearium, Miller created scores of paintings and drawings and developed new special effects and photographic techniques. His last project before leaving the museum was a 10'x12' mural of Jupiter as seen from one of its moons. He is now a free-lance illustrator and was among the artists invited to document the Apollo-Soyuz launch in 1975.

Miller's astronomical work is seen in many publications, such as *Analog, Starlog, Future, Smithsonian, Science News*. He does wildlife illustrations as well, and is currently illustrating a fantasy novel. Several of his original paintings are in the permanent collection of the Smithsonian Institution, as well as in private collections.

He lives with Judith Miller and three cats in Woodbridge, Virginia.          □